Pennsylvania Ghosts and Haunts
*West Pennsylvania*

ISBN: 978-1-940087-43-6
21 Crows Dusk to Dawn Publishing, 21 Crows, LLC

Disclaimer: The stories and legends in this book are for enjoyment purposes and taken from many different resources. Many have been passed down and have been altered along the way. I attempt to sort through the many different variations found on a story and find the most popular and the most supported by historical evidence/verbal interviews. Not all sources and legends can be substantiated. Public properties may become private after the printing of the book or they may simply be listed with the address so you know the historical area where the story originated. Listing the GPS and address does not mean you can visit. Regardless if the area is listed as private or not, please respect the landowner and do not disturb their privacy, nor trespass. Readers assume full responsibility for use of information in this book. Please use common sense.

Front Cover: Polly Williams of White Rock and Moll Derry
Back Cover: Dead Man's Hollow

I0552038

## Table of Contents

*Parking:*

**Blue Mist Trail**

*377 Irwin Road*

*Gibsonia, PA 15044*

*40.625514, -80.006635*

*To (about 1.4 mile walk)*

*Parking:*

*Irwin Road*

*Gibsonia, PA 15044*

*40.607557, -80.000886*

## Legend of Blue Mist Road

The trail near the intersection of Jackson and Irwin roads. Do not let the encouraging nature trail signs fool you—it may be an ominous journey ahead. For example, center to the image might be a hanging tree. And that is only a few steps in—

One of Pittsburgh's most haunted roads is Blue Mist Road in the North Hills. The hiking section is blocked from traffic, runs about 1.4 miles from a turnoff of Babcock Road to Jackson/Irwin Road, and offers an isolated path created from an old roadway paralleling the sometimes-swampy Irwin Run.

Deep in the woods of Blue Mist Road where lost souls lurk.

The roadway has been there since at least the early 1900s. Along its route, there were a few homes with long driveways leading to their back doors. This section of Irwin Road is now blocked off and run by the Allegheny Land Trust preserved for a hiking trail. You do not need to walk far off a little pull-off on Jackson Road where the cold air hits the warm to get a ghostly feel. The creek lets off a foggy mist that wiggles its way through a pocket of the forest and along the lonely path.

There are stories of dark shadows following trekkers along the old roadbed. When approached, they fade away. Some might think it had gotten a bad name in the 1970s when newspapers covered a bizarre drug party and a sniper attack along Irwin Road. In March of 1970, an unidentified gunman took two shots at a policeman trying to serve a warrant for a 19-year-old driving on a suspended license. Then on Friday, June 26, 1970, the police received a report of a man dancing naked on Irwin Road. It ended with a teenage girl getting hit by a car (she lived), a dog getting shot because it bit a policeman (it did not live), and a drug bust with minors involved.

Then there have been a few deaths—a 44-year-old man was found leaning against a tree with a gunshot wound to his head in January of 1979, his death considered a hunting mishap. And there have been a couple of wrecks near Babcock Road, one with the fatality of a mother of two young children.

When I walked the road on a dimming evening as winter started in, I had not planned on the untimely dark of night sneaking in at a mere five o'clock. It was a warmer day a week after early winter snow. The mixture caused the fog to rise along the bank at dusk and work its way up the path. It was eerie, surreal. A Great Horned Owl was hoo-hoo-hooing in a low tone in the woods. My camera caught some insects reflecting like orbs in the LCD screen when I peeked to see what ghosts I had captured with my lens. My foggy breath had crept up into the air to look like vaporous spooks in the images I could see. Creepy.

An evening walk along Blue Mist Trail with its ghostly tales leaves very little up to the imagination. Especially with my breath catching in the pictures when I would peek at them.

I began to conjure up some spooks myself. I felt somewhat uneasy walking there and quickened my steps. It is not typical. Maybe it was my imagination running wild with the pictures I was taking. I walk darkened trails all the time without feeling little more than wary of unfamiliar humans I might come upon.

But as the fog gathered me in its grasp, I could not help but recall tales I had read about Blue Mist Road. Many years ago, a young couple had driven along this same secluded road before authorities blocked it for foot traffic. The two worked the car along its rugged path. They had heard the same tales I had been told—of little people who chased teen cars, of shots ringing out from a gun held in phantom hands at those who traversed the isolated road. They, too, had read of the ghostly remnants of Ku Klux Klan lynchings in this neck of the woods and a particularly ancient tree where the ghostly remains of their victims still dangled while wisps of white cloaks circled the knotted trunk. Some have even seen a half-man and half-cow lurking in the shadows and peering into car windows.

On this night, the young couple was looking for the old hanging tree. Twice, they traversed the rugged, gravel-dirt road as the evening left the sky, and the hint of darkness began surrounding all but the tan-orange headlights. Unable to succeed in finding the tree, the two parked the car, letting it idle. They chose a secluded spot near an old driveway overgrown with tall grass leading to what they surely believed could be a buckle-roofed house—a haunted, buckle-roofed house, that is. There they sat and chatted. They watched their breath condensate on the windshield and awaited full darkness along with the mist that witnesses said would creep up around the car along with knotted-knuckled fingers patting on the roof or the glass.

"Okay, here we go—" Then, the boy shut off the car with a simple turn of his fingers to the key and a smug twist of his lips. He swallowed hard, making a show of it, so the girl giggled. "Honk the horn three times," she told him. And so, he did. *Beep-beep-beep.*

"Now, we count to ten," the boy whispered in the silence so deathly that the pressure almost hurt his ears. "And wait for the ghosts to come."

A tree thought to be part of the legend, *the hanging tree.*

*One-two-three—* When the tendrils of fog began to creep up toward the doors, the boy and girl began to count to ten and prepared themselves to join the many before them. They would watch the legend unfold as they started to count, go through the steps, see whatever shades of death would test their courage this night. *Four-five-six—* They counted softly together as the darkness faded farther away on the horizon, and quiet filled the inside of the car. It was exhilarating, this thrill. The mist crawled its way to the windshield, a bluish tone reflecting off the deep turquoise of what little remained of the evening sky. *Seven-eight-nine—*

"Ten," the girl said quietly as the darkness and fog enveloped them. "Now, see if the car starts." The boy chuckled softly and let his hand rise to the ignition. He grasped the still-warm key in his fingers, turning it with great drama, knowing it would start, but enjoying the way the girl tilted nervously forward in her seat in both panic and fascination. *Ching-ching*. But it did not start. Silence.

*Pat-pat*. Something made a soft beat on the roof. The girl's eyes widened. "It's just dew dripping from the trees," the boy said a little too quickly, flaunting his common sense even if his voice was shaky. His heart was racing, startled. Then he brushed the fear off. "Or a branch hitting it." She nodded. But his hands were trembling a bit as he struggled with the key once again. *Ching-ching*.

Finally, after wrestling with the demons in his head of witches and ghosts lurking around outside, the boy decided he would rather battle any wicked creature than deal with the wrath of the girl's father if she was late getting home tonight. He would have to explain why his car broke down on secluded Irwin Road. Surely, it was just frayed wires wet from the muddy road and the tendrils of fog creeping up from the creek and under the hood. He told the girl that and opened the door, stepped out into the darkness. She watched the fog envelop him as soon as he closed the door. The boy disappeared into the mist. She jumped, startled at the boom when he unlatched the hood, and the hinges made a squeaky opening. Then it was quiet again.

*Pat-pat*. She listened to the boy poking around beneath the hood, working his way upward in the engine to find a frayed wire or a busted hose. *Tap-tap*. The girl sat back in the seat, trying not to listen to her heart pounding as it kept rhythm to the taps coming from the roof again. *Tap-tap*.

Time seemed to pass and sluggishly—too slowly for the girl. Had it been five minutes? Or ten? *Tap-tap.* She unrolled the window just a bit and called out the boy's name. Only silence returned. *Tap-tap.* The sound on the roof of the car unnerved her, and she quickly rolled up the window with wide eyes, peering upward as if she could see something through the vinyl and metal.

*Tap-tap.* Now the noise was more irritating than scary. Surely the boy was standing with a stick in his hand, stabbing it at the roof, waiting in the mist, waiting for her to come outside so he could jump out and scare her. "Stop it!" she yelled at the hood, then the window, then the roof. "It isn't funny." *Tap-tap.* But he did not come out.

Finally, in a fit of rage, the girl pushed open the car door and stomped along the muddy ground. She waggled her head, searching for the stick, and instead found her eyes catching on something white dangling just above the roof, almost hidden in the mist. *Tap-tap.* She narrowed her eyes and leaned forward, peering hard into the haze. She pulled up a hand slowly, reluctantly reached out, and poked the white thing with the tip of her forefinger. It was warm and appeared to bob away. The mist parted lazily by her hand, and she squinted where her fingers still lay suspended next to the thing she had touched. Was it—the grubby toe of a tennis shoe? To her utter horror, she could see the pointed toe of a tennis shoe barely touching the roof of the car. *Tap-tap.* She followed it up to a blue-jeaned leg, and then as a bit of mist parted, the boy dangling there with a noose around his neck. The wind wiggled the branch on the tree, and his toe hit the roof. *Tap-tap. Tap-tap—*

**Crossroads Cemetery**
**3261 Wexford Road**
**Gibsonia, PA 15044**
**40.630635, -80.010865**

## Leaning Tombstones

The leaning tombstones. *Image: KSStephens*

At the Crossroads Cemetery, two tombstones lean toward each other, coming closer every year. They belong to a husband and wife, John and Mary Fogal, whose love spread farther than life. After death, they try to be together. As years pass, the graves lean more and more toward each other. At night, their hands reach out through the tombs so they can clasp them until morning.

**Campbells Run Road**
*Pittsburgh, PA 15238*
*40.540214, -79.855636*
*to*
*40.546957, -79.867854*

## 13 Bends Road

Campbells Run Road—a couple bends of the thirteen needed to complete the legend. As usual, check with the county engineer's office or local enforcement agencies if you are not sure if old roads are still accessible to the public.

In Harmar Township, an old unpaved, dirt-rutted road called Campbells Run winds its way through an isolated patch of thick woods. Along the way, there are thirteen curves in the road before it dead-ends where it once met with Old Indian Trail Road. When the road was easily accessible and not blocked by gates or concrete barricades, teens would drive the route and then stop at the last bend.

They would turn off the car and one of the braver of the lot would get out of the car and pat a thin layer of baby powder on the hood before returning to the comfort of the vehicle to await a ghostly event. For a few of the lucky thrill-seekers, after a short time, children's tiny handprints would form where the baby powder had been placed. The story grows even more curious as on the return trip, one of the bends would  disappear. Instead of thirteen, there were then only twelve!

# Dead Man's Hollow Conservation Area

**Parking:** *Boston Ballfield Park*
*1906 Donner Street*
*McKeesport, PA 15135*
*40.310503, -79.830441*
**Dead Man's Hollow: .8 mile trail walk**
*Great Allegheny Passage (North)*
*McKeesport, PA 15135*
*40.317985, -79.840733*

## Dead Man's Hollow

Union Sewer Pipe Company once at Dead Man's Hollow. *Image: McKeesport Regional History & Heritage Center, McKeesport, PA*

There is a dark valley along the Youghiogheny River south of McKeesport. It is just a little less than a mile from the Boston Ballfield Park along the Great Allegheny Passage Youghiogheny River Trail. While trekking beneath the trees along a quiet, meticulously kept pathway, it is hard to imagine that it was a bustling industrial area from the late 1880s to the 1920s. That is until you take a slight detour off the trail into a mysterious, untamed dell. This place is called Dead Man's Hollow, and it has a storied past and a legend.

Dead Man's Run—the creek running through it is littered with remnants of the past—whiskey bottles, old bricks, and clay pipe.

Here amid the underbrush and beside a creek, there are the skeletal ruins of old buildings and a wealth of scraps and discards leftover from days long gone. Those bits and pieces of yesteryears—bricks and clay pipes and occasional bottles—leave clues of the area's past. Over the years, the property has changed hands. It was once a part of the 1881 George Flemming Stone Quarry, where laborers mined the rock for railroad ballast. Evidence of that quarry is still seen today in old wagon trails and sandstone, shale, and limestone rock outcroppings with holes drilled for blasting.

In 1893, the Union Brick & Stone Company purchased the quarry property before selling it in 1898 for use as the Bowman Brick Factory for making bricks and paving blocks. Along with foundations of kilns, their castoffs lie in the dirt and brush easily seen by a keen eye, especially the deep red-orange bricks peeking from the soil. Into the 1920s and for over 30 years, the Union Sewer Pipe Company made sewer pipe, terra cotta, building block, and fire brick and sent them by rail to many cities throughout the U.S.

Ruins of the old industries, including Union Sewer Pipe Company, where many worked and some died.

By then, the area was full of brick machinery, storage buildings, elevators, stone crushers, coal-fired kilns, and derricks, some still present today. You can see parts of the old buildings used and find remnants of the terra cotta pipes knee-deep in the creek. Around 1925, there was an explosion in one of the kilns, and the business shut down. But among the scraps, thick underbrush, and building carcasses, there are a few leftovers from yesteryears that stick out the most in Dead Man's Hollow—and those are its ghosts.

The Youghiogheny River near Dead Man's Hollow. Quiet. Serene. Haunted.

Dead Man's Hollow received its grisly name from the number of corpses that show up along the banks of the Youghiogheny River at this point. It is the perfect dumping site as the river is bent and twisted at an ideal angle here. When the water flows past, anything with weight bobbing within the river's fickle grasp tends to work its way toward the shore and get stuck in the more stagnant water of the bank where a creek—Dead Man's Run—sweeps into it. Those who drown upriver wash up on the shore there.

Not all were brought in by the river, though. A group of boys exploring the woods found a dead body hanging within the hollow in the 1870s along a creek valley. The corpse was so decomposed nobody could identify it. Everybody started calling it "the hollow the dead man showed up." Locals eventually shortened the name to Dead Man's Hollow. And aptly so. Over the years, many have died here. Some say their spirits have not gone away. Here is a collection of a few souls who have departed life near Dead Man's Hollow and might still be lingering today—

**January 15, 1874**—Four men were crossing the Youghiogheny on a breezy day. As a coal barge began to pass, a violent gust of wind hit the barge's side, sweeping it sideways, so it crashed into the smaller boat. Two were able to make a desperate swim to shore. John Colson, who worked as a mechanic for the National Tubes Works, died. The Monongahela Valley Republican reported: *John Colson, a skillful mechanic from the Tube Works, was an excellent swimmer and would have probably saved himself but the other poor fellow, who was an entire stranger, and could not swim, seized him in a death-grip and both went down together.*

**August 2, 1881**—35-year-old George A. McClure was a father of three and co-owner of Hendrickson and McClure's hardware store in 1881. A gang of thieves, including Ward McConkey, burglarized the store. McClure, determined to retrieve the few hundred dollars' worth of stolen goods, set out with two men—Joseph Lynch and George A. Flemming (who owned the property and believed he knew where the robbers had stashed the loot). The three men searched the hollow all day and were unable to find it. Around dusk, they stopped to rest when seven men surrounded them and began to fire. Flemming and Lynch escaped. McClure was found dead around 9:30 p.m., riddled with bullet holes, in the woods at Dead Man's Hollow.

A judge sentenced Ward McConkey to hang on May 1883 for the murder. He claimed innocence to the moment of death. The newspapers reported the 19-year-old declared this before he died: "All I have to say, gentlemen, is that you hang me because you think I know something about the murder of George McClure and won't squeal and the people of McKeesport want to see me hanged, but I'm innocent." A white cap was placed over his face, and just before the trap was sprung, McConkey uttered, "Goodbye, murderers, goodbye."

**March 14, 1883**—Foreman George Henninger, his brother, Daniel, and two other men were preparing for blasting work in the quarry. As they started to organize for the day, one of them noted that the dynamite they would be using had been frozen solid. Despite the setback, one man decided to start a small fire to thaw out a cartridge of the frozen dynamite. George Henninger and Daniel Henninger buddied up to the fire to warm their hands at about the same time that the cartridge exploded. The blast killed at least two men in what one news reporter described as "arms and legs being burned and hurled hither and thither."

**1887**—74-year-old Edward Woods drowned in the Youghiogheny River while riding the McClure Ferry. He lost his footing and toppled over the side of the boat.

**September 25, 1905**—Mike Sacco, employed at Union Sewer Pipe Company, was leaving work. He stepped inside the elevator and tugged on the rope to lower it. Instead, it began to rise, and he made the rash decision to jump off. He was not quick enough. Sacco's body wedged between the second-floor ceiling and the elevator floor, which crushed him to death.

**August 8, 1907**—39-year-old Peter Sandy of the Youghiogheny Brick and Supply died in an explosion of dynamite in the quarry at Dead Man's Hollow.

**December 1, 1916**—Two hunters, following the baying of a hound they believed had tracked a rabbit, found the corpse of 40-year-old Samuel Candy of Braddock partially submerged in a creek in Dead Man's Hollow. Candy had disappeared the previous Tuesday after leaving work from the Edgar Thomson Steel Works. In a postmortem exam, Dr. Porter of McKeesport found three bullets in the small of the man's back, one in the neck, one on his left side, one in the right shoulder, one in the breast, and one under the right arm.

The Pittsburgh Post-Gazette made this statement: *Mr. Candy had interpreted many cases at the Braddock Police Station, and the police believe that he was the victim of enemies who thought he was betraying them to the authorities.* A second motive may have been love. Candy was courting a woman from Wilmerding when another suitor came along and began threatening him "with violence."

Dead Man's Run—the creek where a dead man was found, and perhaps his ghost still lingers.

**May 26, 1944**—A married couple and a couple who were to be betrothed were returning to their home in Dead Man's Hollow via a small rowboat on the Youghiogheny. Because it was overloaded, one of the men was swimming alongside the boat. Midstream, a gust of wind before an oncoming storm overturned the boat. The three within spilled into the depths of the river. The two women, one 33-years-old and the other only 20-years-old drowned.

Oh, and then there was mention of a monstrous snake: **August 1893**—A man named Charles Brown was walking along the Youghiogheny River at Dead Man's Hollow, and before him, a giant snake appeared. He fainted, collapsing to the dirt. When he arose again, the snake was gone.

## TWENTY-FIVE FEET LONG.

---

### The Monster Snake That Is Stirring Up a Community.

MCKEESPORT, PA., Aug. 4.—The big snake said to exist in this vicinity has once more been seen. Messrs. John Cox, Harry Filder, Thomas Clennendson and others who composed a berry party, saw the big reptile, and were raced quite a distance by it.

The party almost walked upon his snake-ship this morning, at 6 o'clock, at Deadman's Hollow. They were badly frightened, and claim that the snake was almost 25 feet in length. It made for the party with mouth wide open. The snake has been seen by 25 people of this city, but few credit the stories told.

Pittsburgh Dispatch—AUGUST 5, 1891

A most intriguing story comes from a 1934 sighting by Michael Bendzuch Jr., a resident of Dead Man's Hollow, one moon-lit night. While Bendzuch crossed the Youghiogheny on a rowboat, he watched in wonder as a thin layer of fog began to float across the riverbank. Then, a silhouette favoring an Indian swept from the mist and stopped to stand along the shore, seemingly as interested in the young man on the boat as the young man was curious about the eerie presence. They both stared across the water for what seemed like an eternity before the old ghost stories told to him as a young child flittered past Bendzuch's mind. Quickly, he gave the shoreline a wide berth just as the mist and the ghost vanished.

The Allegheny Land Trust is now caring for this unique piece of history, land, and the legends that come with it. It has embraced the natural beauty and its celebrated past, opening it up for everyone to explore. Those discovering its ghostly side will not be disappointed. Witnesses have heard a baby's sob within on full-moon nights, crying for whoever was murdered by the hanging in the hollow.

The trail just outside Dead Man's Hollow. Enter at your own risk because there are ghosts here. (This trail is accessible for wheelchairs too —you may have to be a little adventurous with some pea-gravel, and you will have to stop outside the ruins about right here, but during the autumn, you can view the buildings and the river and perhaps, see a ghost!)

There are reports of shadow figures lingering in the woods and along the trail, the sound of low talking even though no one else is around. Just remember, though, those ghosts may not be tame—it was a hideout for gangs and thugs and people who died violently and might hold a grudge because, well, you are still alive. One of the spirits lingering there is none other than Ward McConkey, who hanged in May 1883 for the murder of hardware store owner George McClure. He is out for vengeance because even on that scaffold, he denied he was the killer. So, if you are standing there some dark evening, and you hear this whispered in your ear: "Goodbye, murderers, goodbye." Run. Because you might end up another ghost in that hollow!

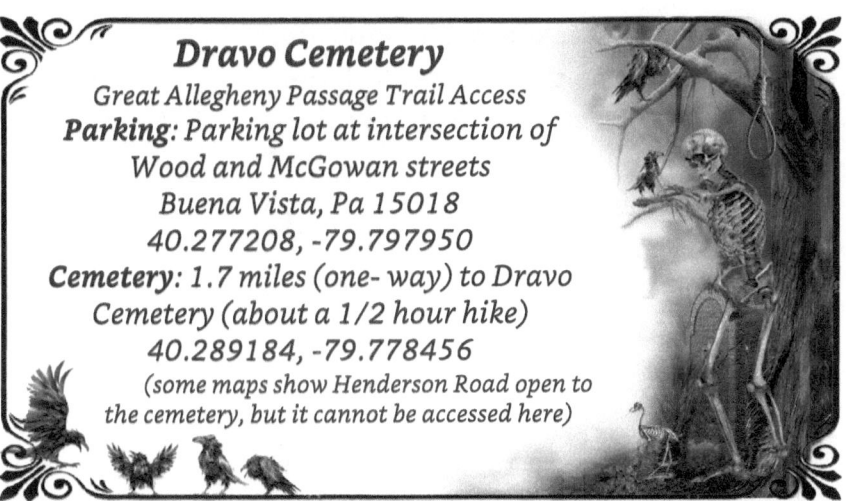

### Dravo Cemetery

*Great Allegheny Passage Trail Access*
**Parking:** *Parking lot at intersection of*
*Wood and McGowan streets*
*Buena Vista, Pa 15018*
*40.277208, -79.797950*
**Cemetery:** *1.7 miles (one-way) to Dravo*
*Cemetery (about a 1/2 hour hike)*
*40.289184, -79.778456*
*(some maps show Henderson Road open to*
*the cemetery, but it cannot be accessed here)*

## Two-Headed Dog and a Phantom Train at Dravo Cemetery

The old railway bed, *left*, now a hiking trail with a phantom train. There was once a church only feet off the tracks.
*Right*, there is still a cemetery—one haunted by a two-headed dog and ghosts who stand by their graves.

A two-headed dog haunts an old graveyard along an isolated section of railroad tracks not far from Dead Man's Hollow. Although the cause of the dog's appearance has never been explained, some believe two-headed creatures can see into this world and the world of the dead.

The cemetery itself is like any other. It is an old one dating back to the time when William Newlin, a farmer in the late 1700s, set aside a grassy hillock overlooking the river for a quiet location to use as a family burial ground. It was not long after and in the mid-1800s that coal mining towns began to pop up nearby, including nearby Stringtown—so named for the string or series of homes along the roadway.

Where the Methodist Church once stood and just beyond the tree, the railway where sparks were sent from trains that caught the church on fire—twice. A phantom train is heard blasting along the tracks complete with a spine-chilling whistle.

As farming and mining opportunities increased in the area, so too did the population. Noting that the community needed a place of worship, Reverend William Dravo, who was close friends with the Newlin family, sought permission to erect a church on their property. Approval was granted, and churchgoers built a two-story Methodist Church next to the family cemetery in 1824. They expanded the burial plot to also take in the dead of the community.

By 1882, the Pittsburgh and Lake Erie Railroad had developed a line along the Youghiogheny River and through the little hamlet as it made its way from Pittsburgh through Connellsville. The communities around it would grow and, along with them, the members of the church and the number of graves in the cemetery. And it would probably still be here today, a lone memorial for the towns that once stood except the building burned down twice before folks realized sparks from the trains passing close by started the fires. The parishioners never rebuilt the second time. By the 1930s, the industries in the area began to wane, and the cemetery was so overgrown, the graves were hardly noticeable.

The cemetery runs toward the river. Ghostly shadows are seen standing near the graves.

Now, all that remains of the long-gone coal town along the river, barring the trail, modern public restroom, picnic shelter, and campsite—are the stones of those buried there that were gently restored during the 1990s by a scout group. But as the cemetery became more accessible to hikers and bikers, witnesses began seeing a two-headed dog lurking about the graveyard.

The first reported sighting was from a group of scouts who had gotten permission to camp near the old graveyard one night. While on a light-hearted foray to check for ghosts at the cemetery, howls burst into the air in the darkness of night, and the boys scurried back to the camp with fearful excitement, daring to divulge they had seen a two-headed dog with red eyes bounding from behind one of the headstones. Others attest to the strange dog. It appears and disappears or leaves a mournful cry echoing through the hills.

Those biking past have also witnessed shadows standing near the graves. A few visitors to the area also claim to feel a rush of wind along the tracks, hear the grind of steel wheels on the rail, and see the eerie outline of a ghost train looming in the distance—perhaps the spirited remnants of a busy railway's past.

## Montour Trail
**Parking: Montour Trail—National Tunnel**
*Off McConnell Road, Canonsburg, PA 15317*
*Cecil, PA 15321*
*40.315774, -80.187912*
*(Tunnel: 40.317075, -80.182664)*
**Parking: Montour Trail—Greer Tunnel**
*Off Linwood Avenue/Buckeye Street*
*McMurray, PA 15317*
*40.300826, -80.122183*
*(Tunnel: 40.297116, -80.129396)*

## Colorful Old Railway Ghosts—
### Little Green Wraith with Glowing Red Eyes and a Ghost Girl in a White Dress

The Montour Trail—for those who like to bike, run, hike, or seek out a ghost or two.

The Montour Railroad was built between 1877 to 1914, connecting the Pittsburgh and Lake Erie Railroad with numerous other railway systems and over 30 coal mines. It was eventually abandoned but reopened as a hike/bike path that stretches over 60 miles around Pittsburgh.

The Montour Tunnel—a great starting point if you like a long hike on a rail-trail. The trail between this tunnel and the Greer Tunnel is haunted.

Tunnels along the Montour Trail include the 623-foot-long National Tunnel by Hendersonville, named for the nearby National Coal Company mines. Both ends of the passageway have been sealed off with flaps as large icicles are known to form in the tunnel, but it is accessible.

Another tunnel about 3.9 hiking miles away is known as Bells Tunnel, Montour Tunnel, or Greer Tunnel, which is 235 feet long. Mysterious deaths surround it—in May of 1885, a falling boulder killed two of seven men working in the tunnel. On a hot and windless July night in 1912, an old maple tree on the Bell farm nearby fell on a tent pitched under it, killing two 19-year-old campers.

The trail between the two tunnels has a ghostly presence. Some who walk it feel a sense of unease in certain areas. A little ghost girl in a white dress walks the trail. Another wraithlike form is a bit creepier—a tiny apparition with green eyes and one white hand.

**Green Man Tunnel**
*3898 Piney Fork Road*
*South Park Township, Pennsylvania*
**Parking:** *40.272567, -79.969801*
**Tunnel:** *40.272693, -79.969310*

## Legend of Green Man Tunnel/Charlie No-Face

The legendary Green Man Tunnel —South Park Township. A part of a legend that still lives on.

On the outskirts of Pittsburgh, the Pennsylvania Railroad's Peters Creek Branch followed Peters Creek and serviced coal mines between Large to Snowden. Along its route and near the place where the smaller Piney Fork spills into Peters Creek, the trains traveled through a tunnel that would become a part of one of Pennsylvania's most celebrated urban legends.

The story goes something like this: *An electrician from Dravosburg was out working in a remote area in the late evening on power lines at the top of the tunnel. As he worked the wires, he was suddenly given a violent jolt and was thrown from his perch and killed almost instantly. When they found the dead man later that night, his skin had turned bright green from the electrocution, and it glowed in the dusky air. Afterward, those visiting the tunnel could pull up and turn off their headlights. If they called out his name, he would appear as a green, glowing figure from within the tunnel. For some, he would touch the car, and the electric shock would make the vehicle stall, and it may not restart.*

It is not often that an urban legend this far-fetched is based on a true story. But the lore surrounding the elusive Green Man can be traced, as many folktales do, to another location miles away and to a little boy named Raymond Robinson. And it is more horrifying than even the urban legend spawned from it.

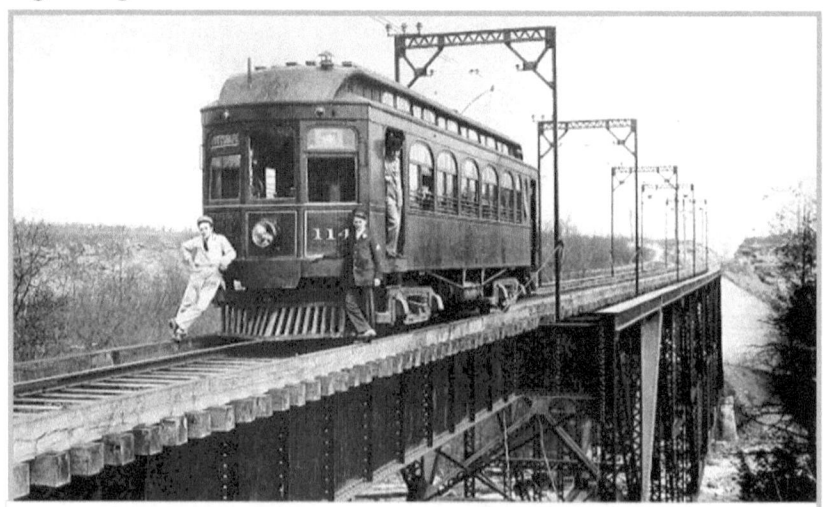

Where the legend began—the Harmony short line, an electric streetcar route of the Beaver Valley Traction Company.

The story began on a warm Wednesday, June 18th, 1919, when 8-year-old Raymond, whose family lived in Morado, and four of his friends headed to a local swimming hole.

As they came upon the Morado Bridge, he took a dare and clambered up to the top of a pole reaching for a bird's nest settled there. The pole was along the Harmony short line, an electric streetcar route of the Beaver Valley Traction Company. Unexpectedly, his hand had come to rest on a lightning arrester, and 11,000 nearly deadly volts shot into his body. There was a single blinding flash before the jolt flung the boy toward the ground.

He hovered between life and death for weeks. Where his eyes had been, there were only sockets, his nose was gone, and his mouth was just a hole, making any speech difficult to understand. He lost a hand burned almost to his elbow, and he nearly lost his life. But Raymond Robinson did not lose his sense of adventure nor his kindness even though his appearance startled people.

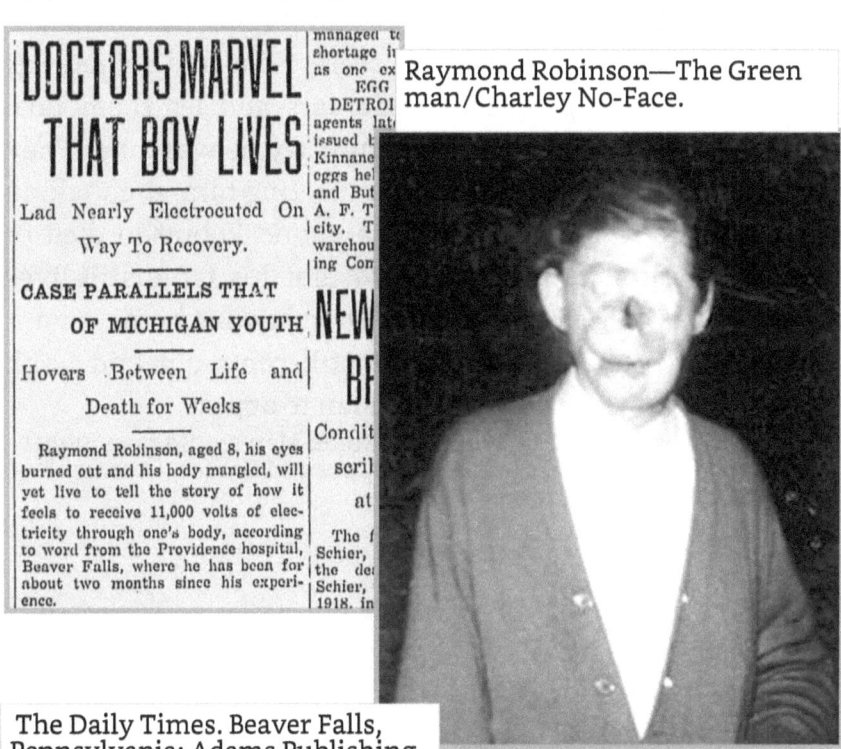

**DOCTORS MARVEL THAT BOY LIVES**

Lad Nearly Electrocuted On Way To Recovery.

**CASE PARALLELS THAT OF MICHIGAN YOUTH**

Hovers Between Life and Death for Weeks

Raymond Robinson, aged 8, his eyes burned out and his body mangled, will yet live to tell the story of how it feels to receive 11,000 volts of electricity through one's body, according to word from the Providence hospital, Beaver Falls, where he has been for about two months since his experience.

Raymond Robinson—The Green man/Charley No-Face.

The Daily Times. Beaver Falls, Pennsylvania: Adams Publishing Group. August 4, 1919.

As he grew up, Raymond did become somewhat of a recluse, spending much of his time listening to the radio. During the day, he worked at home, making wallets and doormats to sell. At night, he found consolation in the quiet hikes he would take after dark when he thought few would see him. During his life, he would walk Koppel-New Galilee Road (Route 351) alone and at night, despite his family's resistance and fear for his safety. He used a stick to guide himself and one foot on the road, so he knew what direction he should take. It was not long before passersby began to take a shocking note of the unusual man caught momentarily in their headlights.

The 1950s and 1960s were the height of his popularity with curiosity-seekers. For decades, teens would drive the road searching for a glimpse of Raymond, who they dubbed *Green Man* due to the way his clothing reflected in the car lights, or *Charlie No-Face* for his scars. He would sometimes stop and talk to people in their cars and let them take pictures of him. Those who met him say he was kind. They love to recall the fond memory of meeting him, then taking their friends to meet him too. Raymond Robinson died in 1984 of natural causes at age 74. But his fame still lives outside Pittsburgh in more areas than just his hometown— Green Man Tunnel. Where folks still come out and honk their horn, waiting for the Green Man to appear.

The actual road (PA-351) where the Green Man would take nightly walks for about 30 years between Koppel and Galilee, 50 miles north of Green Man Tunnel.

**Restland Memorial Park**
*2319 Johnston Road*
*Monroeville, PA 15146*
*40.411213, -79.801574*

## Walkin' Rosie/Roamin' Rosie

Restland Memorial Park—once home to a roaming statue.

There was once a statue at the Restland Memorial Cemetery that would move forward when a flashlight shined upon it. Although cemetery caretakers removed the statue, the woman who was buried beneath the headstone now returns in ghostly form. She floats around the cemetery in a white gown.

## Braddock's Field
*Jones Avenue*
*North Braddock, PA 15112*
*Along Braddock's Road to*
*Marker for Center of Battlefield:*
*40.402956, -79.863320*

### Braddock's Gold

Braddock's Fall. General Braddock was defeated on the banks of the Monongahela and he died. His ghost may not be there, but his treasure might. *Image: The New York Public Library*.

Turtle Creek is a stream in Pennsylvania. It begins in Delmont and runs its course a little over 21 miles, and eventually spills whatever contents it has claimed along its route into the Monongahela River. As far as folklore goes, that creek would not stand out any more than any of the other major streams flowing into the Monongahela—except that it has a major historical event nearby attached with a legendary treasure.

At the juncture where it meets with the Monongahela, the British army fought a force of Indians and French in the summer of 1755. British General Braddock was heading along with 2400 soldiers toward Fort Duquesne, located at the confluence of the Monongahela and the Allegheny Rivers, in a military expedition to invade the fort. Among his men was a Virginia militia officer named George Washington and a foot soldier, Daniel Boone. He had started from Fort Cumberland in Maryland and headed toward the Monongahela River in Pennsylvania. His goal was to take three critical forts beginning with Duquesne. But to get there, his troops had to spend months cutting a path ten to twelve feet wide and big enough for horse-drawn wagons to plow through an old Lenape Indian trail. The soldiers even complained about the slow slog, leveling even the smallest hill and building bridges over creeks that were shallow enough to navigate without the extra work. The soldiers were worn out—barely surviving on what wild game they could shoot and snake meat.

A section of Braddock's Trail remains at Fort Necessity in Farmington, Pennsylvania.

At the mouth of Turtle Creek, Braddock's forces were ambushed on July 9th, 1755, just as they crossed the river by an irregular army of Canadians and American Indians, whose marksmanship and intimidation tactics proved lethal. Musket fire and war whoops rang out, disorienting Braddock's men, and they fell into disarray. They lost all discipline, and it was a slaughter. Two of every three British soldiers who had crossed the Monongahela that day were killed or wounded within just a few hours. General Braddock was killed, dying four days after the battle, and his forces retreated. The land would come to be called Braddock's Field. And the campaign, the Battle of the Monongahela.

It has often been told his men spoke of General Braddock bringing chests of gold along with him, which he would use to buy equipment and supplies for his troops. If a battle should erupt, he demanded that his soldiers bury the gold quickly as not to come into enemy hands. Some believe that Braddock sent the money back as a letter found in the 1960s mentioned the funds, carried in a 2-wheeled cart called a tumbrel, may have been returned at Cumberland. Others believe it might still be buried somewhere between Cumberland and Turtle Creek, where it spills into the Monongahela.

If you would like to search out the gold, good luck. Most of the battlefield is on private or federally protected lands—under homes and businesses as it encompasses Braddock and North Braddock in Pennsylvania and then, far beyond. But there are still remnants of that road here and there. Others have tried to explore the possibilities. Perhaps you will be the one to find it—

**Edgar Thomson Steel Works
And Port Perry
Old Hamburg Road**
*Braddock Avenue
North Braddock, PA 15112
40.391528, -79.848270
The Old Hamburg Road/tunnel
is not accessible and on private
property. Only for site reference.*

## Old Hamburg Road Ghost

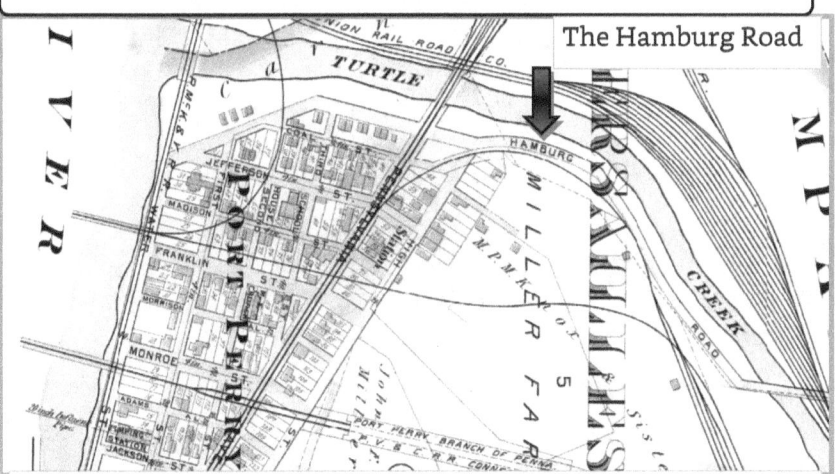

The Hamburg Road

Port Perry at the confluence of Turtle Creek and the Monongahela River. The Hamburg Road was home to a ghost.

Port Perry once stood at the mouth of Turtle Creek in the corner of North Versailles along the Monongahela River. It began its existence on an old hickory lot with only eight families around 1840 and when Braddock was still little more than a forest. Then, a coal mine was there, and flatboats carried the coal downriver.

Lock and Dam #2 were also here at the time, and once the superintendent's house went up, other homes popped up around it. Almost anywhere someone could build a house, it was built, including between sets of railroad tracks and a railroad bridge. The town prospered with a post office that was much-used by the boatmen to get their mail. It also had a sawmill where workers made nearly two million gunstocks for the Civil War, a church, railroad, coal mine, boatyard, grocery, and thirteen saloons. In the 1860s, it boasted over 3,500 residents.

Port Perry about 1916.

Port Perry had its amusing incidents. In 1888, local authorities ruled that the locks would shut on Sundays, barring the mail run or a coal boat rise. Captain Wood, who was the superintendent in charge of the lock then, would not bend at these regulations. One day, a steamboat captain with a tow of empty barges boasted to his peers that maybe nobody else could get through on Sundays, but he certainly would! He was a stubborn man, and even as the navigation officers told him it would never happen, the captain set his sights on Wood's lock.

As the lock was closed on Sunday, the steamboat captain sent word to Wood that he would be coming through—he had an emergency trip and needed to make it that day. He received a message in return that they certainly would not open until after midnight—the rules were clearly laid out, and there were few exceptions. The captain, too, would have to follow the rules. Wood would make no concession even in a meeting. Such, the steamboatman replied during the most heated part of the conversation: "All right then, I'll make things pleasant for you during the day if I am compelled to stay."

Wood's house, at the time, was just across the street. The steamboat captain pulled the whistle wide and let out a blast as if to warn the superintendent that the battle was not over. When Wood refused to change his mind, the whistle was turned on from nine o'clock on Sunday morning until midnight, never ceasing its incessant howls and shrieks and bellows of all kinds. It was still not until after midnight that he was able to make his way through the lock!

Later and in the early 1870s, Andrew Carnegie would build his steel mill next door, and as the towns around Port Perry grew, the once-bustling port seemed to languish a bit. In 1923, the steel mill grew and cut off much of the little town's access. The only way in and out was a tunnel under the mill leading to the old dirt Hamburg Road on the edge of town.

This tunnel was the object of many ghost stories—what folks called the Port Perry Tunnel along the Hamburg Road. As one story goes, a woman was murdered in the tunnel during the 1920s. Bereft at the loss, her husband threw himself beneath a train. After, a white figure would emerge at the tunnel and road with shining eyes frightening even the most dauntless walkers.

Port Perry, left. Edgar Thomson, right. Turtle Creek is center.
*Image: Library of Congress*

This particular story may be loosely based on the murder of Julia (Conroy) Coyne. At 8:00 a.m. on the morning of July 18th, 1923, John Conroy, the girl's father, tried desperately to find the young 18-year-old at her little unpainted shack in Port Perry she shared with her new husband, 36-year-old Patrick Coyne. The father had frantically come from the family home in Braddock to notify Julia, said to be quite beautiful with auburn hair and a slim build, there was a dire emergency. Her new husband of just a few months, a railroad brakeman, had fallen beneath two freight cars in the South Duquesne yards where he was employed. Doctors amputated his legs in emergency surgery. John Conroy was also understandably spurred on by a simple act of kindness by Coyne, who had reached into his pocket before surgery and pulled out his last twenty-dollar bill to give to Julia should he die.

John Conroy banged on the couple's door, then knocked on the windows. When nobody answered, he was alarmed.

Conroy snatched up a stick and broke the door window, then reached inside and turned the knob. After a frantic search of the house, he found his daughter's battered and bare body on the bed. She was bruised, cold, and dead. The coroner estimated that her corpse had laid there 12 hours.

Port Perry. *Image: Library of Congress*

Suspicion fell on Coyne from the start. When Julia's father had initially called to find her at work where she should have been, staff told him that she had not shown up for her housekeeping job at Braddock Hotel. A note had been sent by her husband stating she was ill. Neighbors reported that Coyne had oddly visited the house several times during the day. Then Police found that her husband had inquired at the hotel where she worked if Julia had gone out the night before, and the proprietor stated that yes, she had tagged along with him and his wife.

Coyne was known to be jealous and had beaten his wife on several occasions. Julia would leave him, then return in a few days. Initially, the only evidence was a bloody fingerprint on a mantel and a rosary on her arm as if pleading for her life just before death. There was a recently purchased .38 caliber revolver found at the scene, along with money and jewelry ruling out a robbery gone wrong.

Strangely, Coyne had forgotten his lantern that he always took for his 3:00 to 11:00 shift when he went to work that afternoon. Then, on July 23rd, in the home the couple shared, they found a pair of bloody trousers known to be those Patrick Coyne wore the day before Julia's father discovered her body. Empty shells belonging to the gun were found in the fire grate, and more cartridges from the gun were found in Coyne's jacket in the closet. Fellow employees at the railyard also disclosed that Coyne had divulged that he "was tired of living" the day he was injured.

Edgar Thomson Steel. Port Perry at rear.

Coyne revealed later that he shot Julia when they wrestled for the gun during a fight. He was charged with her murder and sent to jail. Police never found out if he threw himself beneath the train out of remorse or for sympathy if he got caught. Around March 16, 1927, authorities sent the murderer to Fairview State Hospital for the Criminally Insane for "mental derangement." He died there a few months later, on November 20th of that year.

The Catholic church denied Julia a funeral and rites because she married Coyne out of her faith utilizing a Justice of the Peace. Seven brothers and sisters and her parents attended her small service. It is the perfect mix for a ghost story—a beautiful girl murdered by a madman then not allowed passage to heaven. And, of course, a dead demented man's ghost on the loose. Not long after, passersby began seeing the ghostly form of a man along old Hamburg Road that ran the course of about where Braddock Road is now and along Turtle Creek until it met with the town of Port Perry.

Edgar Thomson blast furnaces. *Image: Library of Congress*

Some are not so convinced that the ghost originates from the murder of the woman. In 1955, Joe Smonski was a maintenance clerk at Edgar Thomson mill. He and a friend were walking the dirt Hamburg Road around 10:00 at night, where it became the railroad tunnel beneath the mill. Before them, a man appeared, carrying a big umbrella. As they got closer, the eyes shone eerily, and the two men left quickly. Others would see the ghost too, either donning an umbrella or wearing a hat. The one thing it had in common in the early years was that it stuck to Hamburg Road.

Edgar Thomson blast furnace. *Image: Library of Congress*

Then, the road changed to accommodate the steel mill. Around February 11th of 1967, one of the workers at Edgar Thomson Steel had a frightening experience. A ghost appeared while he was working at the No 16 Furnace. He described the figure as "darkish white, about 5 feet, 11 inches tall, and standing at the top of the stairway. It had no face but sort of a head resting on its shoulders, and it stood about seven inches off the ground." Immediately after, the man ran to get another steelworker, and he saw it too.

There certainly have been many deaths in that area, and everyone seems to have their idea of who it is. Some trace the ghost(s) to a man killed in the mill—he had jumped into a cinder ladle and died. Soldiers died nearby during Braddock's battle, and there was a steamboat explosion in the river. There were two 21-year-old workers killed at Stack J overcome with furnace gas in 1905 and a worker in 1955 who turned on a mill while another was fixing blades. I like to think the ghost is a Port Perry resident who walked around town and still does in ghostly form. But, it might be something more sinister—a murderer or madman or a steam boatman waiting for another way to get back at a long-gone lock captain that would not let him pass.

**South Side Flats**
*(Old East and West Birmingham)*
*East Carson Street*
*Pittsburgh, PA 15203*
*40.428600, -79.973699*

## The South Side Ghosts

South Side Flats had its own ghost in the 1880s. Right—Old East and West Birmingham in the 1870s and 1880s (until 1872 when the area became dubbed South Flats) that was once one of the larger communities across from Pittsburgh. *Image: LOC*

In the 1880s, on nights when clouds overshadowed the moon around 12:30 a.m., a ghostly man would walk the streets of Birmingham. He was always shrouded in a dark cloak and big slouch hat and creeped up from near the river.

East on Carson Street. *Image: Pittsburgh City Photographer Collection*

He moved quickly along Carson Street before turning abruptly into an empty field, there only to disappear. Behind him, an old mangy and gaunt deerhound would follow, walking with a heavy limp. The dog wore a collar, and from it, a chain dragged behind. People who passed would try to greet the man, but he refused to answer. One man even tossed a stone at the dog to get its attention. He thought it had hit the ribs as the stone disappeared into its shadowy body, but the dog did not flinch or growl and gave no clue he noticed. Strangely, other animals nearby would take no notice of the man or hound.

## Long Gone Jones & Laughlin Steel
*SouthSide Works Cinema*
*425 Cinema Drive*
*Pittsburgh, PA 15203*
*40.427907, -79.964020*

## The Legend of Jim Grabowski and Two Shop

Part of the Old 24th Ward with St. Peter Church, center, and beyond J & L Steel (begun as American Iron Co in 1852). Now home to buildings like waterfront hotels, a cinema, and parking garages, and lingering ghostly evidence of industries of its past. *Image: Historic Pittsburgh*

Jones & Laughlin Steel was in the South Side's East Birmingham neighborhood of Pittsburgh. It produced only iron in the early years, but after 1886, it began making steel. By the time of World War II and in its heyday, they were the fourth-largest producer of steel in the world with over 45,000 workers. It was a massive complex of buildings—encompassing both sides of the Monongahela River with one side for pig iron blast furnaces and the other, open-hearth for producing steel.

One building stands out among the rest as ghostly—it is the Two Shop (named for the number of its open hearth), opened in 1905 and closed in 1960. During the time it was opened, nearly forty employees died there. Some who worked there believed ghosts haunted the Two Shop. Even if they were not a bit wary of spirits, there was superstition involved with a place that had so many deaths.

Occasionally, riggers had to go in Two Shop to move or set up equipment. Of all the workers who dreaded entering the building, it was these men because, according to mill lore, there was a worker named Jim Grabowski who tripped over some equipment a rigger had left behind there. This mishap made him fall into a ladle of molten steel in the 1920s, which killed him instantly. Such, his vengeful ghost was particularly fond of picking on riggers.

Jones & Laughlin Steel Corporation—showing a ladle pouring molten steel into an open-hearth furnace. Although the name of *Jim Grabowski* may not be the worker's real name, it has been used since the 1920s to identify the ghost. *Image: Historic Pittsburgh*

According to custom, if a man died in a ladle, the whole device would be taken away and buried in a byproduct area.

All would have been fine, except many years later, while putting in pipes, the ladle with Jim Grabowski's remains was dug up and had to be cut away with welding tools. They believe that Jim's soul was stuck tight inside the molten steel up to that point. When they dug the ladle up and cut it open, workers released his angry spirit.

Jones & Laughlin Steel Corporation—A ladle like the one that held the ghost at Two Shop. *Image: Historic Pittsburgh*

Such Jim did return to haunt more than a few of those riggers just out of spite for this inconvenience of leaving their equipment lying around. Workers would hear calls for help, but upon turning with wide eyes and readying for another cry of alarm and some horrific accident to a coworker, no one would be present. Immediately after, there was haunting, mocking laughter. Some heard groans but could find no source for the noise.

The mill is long gone. Atop the building are shops and SouthSide Works Cinema. Might ol' Jim be haunting them now, too? Only time will tell.

### Long Gone Jones & Laughlin Steel And Tunnel Park
Pittsburgh, PA 15203
40.428399, -79.964806

## Slag Pile Annie

Tunnel running beneath Jones & Laughlin Steel when the mill was still open where a ghost called Slag Pile Annie was seen. Now, there is a park above the tracks—Tunnel Park. You can take a walk in Tunnel Park, perhaps run into Slag Pile Annie.

Tunnels ran under the Jones & Laughlin Steel blast furnaces allowing trains on the Pittsburgh and Lake Erie Railroad to bypass the mill. An old woman would be seen in the tunnel by workers. When addressed, she would return replies. Once, when rebuffed for being in such a dangerous place, she replied: "I can't get killed. I'm already dead." The workers named the ghost Slag Pile Annie.

### Three Rivers Heritage Trail Near the Old Grays Alley
Near the Ninth Street/Rachel
Carson Bridge
Pittsburgh, PA 15212
40.447850, -80.000055
.6 mile walk along the Three
Rivers Heritage Trail

## The Unrest of Missus Grinder, Arch Murderess and Ghost

Allegheny City—now Pittsburgh's North Side around the time the ghost of a serial killer walked the shores.

Many years ago, a ghost appeared near the old Hand Street Bridge, now Ninth Street Bridge/Rachel Carson Bridge. She wore dark clothing and shuffled past, seeming oblivious of those who stared in horror at her. The reason for her appearance is explained like this—

Martha Grinder, her husband George, a coal miner, and their one-year-old child moved from Louisville to Pittsburgh in 1859. Although at first, they lived in a tiny abode near the Point and by all appearances were rather poor, in just a few months, the family found a place in a finer setting in what is now Pittsburgh's North Side along the Allegheny River. It was then in Gray's Alley just off Hand Street and just above Hand Street Bridge. At the time, this section of Pittsburgh was a separate area of the municipality and known as Allegheny City.

The streets Martha Grinder would walk to care for her neighbors in Allegheny City—looking down Anderson Street to what would have been Hand Street Bridge in the background at the time she was living—heading toward the City of Pittsburgh's business district.

MARTHA GRINDER.

Martha Grinder.

Suddenly, Martha Grinder was donning fashionable clothing, carrying money, and introducing herself to a higher society. If anyone asked of her new prosperity, she told them she was bequeathed a sum of money from a wealthy uncle upon the birth of her child. Martha quickly let herself be known as a hospitable woman and swift to come to the aid of a sick neighbor. One of her most significant characteristics was her tenderness for bereaved families. Most thought her to be kind-hearted, caring, and soft-natured—the first to pat a gentle hand on those who were ill or volunteer her services for care.  Strangely, though, the patients under her care passed away.

Doctors could not explain the deaths; the illnesses were not life-threatening. When they died, Martha was right there in the front row at the funeral, a comfort to the family mourning their dead. She marveled in laying out the body of someone who had passed, preparing the corpse for burial, which was accepted because certainly, no one else wanted to dress their departed.

Martha lived next door to James and Mary Carothers, and not long after they had moved in, Mary became ill. Of course, Martha quickly stepped in to care for Mary, whose health worsened as the days passed instead of getting better. Mary died on August 1, 1865, and after recognizing that James had also taken ill during the time Martha was there, suspicions began to arise. Someone suspected Martha placed poison in both Mary and James' food. The coroner completed an autopsy on the dead woman, and suddenly, it all came to light. Martha Grinder had been poisoning her patients. Powdered arsenic was her means of murder—sprinkled on toast, spooned into warm soup, or added to a cup of soothing milk. Martha had also been stealing from the homes of those she had tended.

Police arrested Martha on August 26, 1865. She confessed to the killings of Mary Carothers and a girl named Jane R. Buchanan (occurring on February 28, 1864), who was a new servant at Martha's home. Jane Buchanan had just begun to work for Martha and, being quite frugal, had collected a large sum of money. She suddenly became ill with violent vomiting and soon died. Martha Grinder quickly called for her trunk of belongings and received them. But when the family came to care for the woman's body, the jewelry, money, and clothing had disappeared. Not wanting any further inquiries, Martha offered her clothing to dress the corpse. After the funeral, the family brought this to the coroner's attention, who did not pursue the questions deeming the woman's death due to natural causes. The police did not investigate the case until after the coroner discovered poison in Mary Carothers's body.

Martha refused to admit she had poisoned others, including her husband's brothers, for reasons of escalating the chance of a more considerable inheritance—Jeremiah, who had passed on November 15, 1864, and Samuel, who had died on December 4, 1864. There was also Marguerite Smith, who was another neighbor and Mary Carothers's sister. Martha told shocked jurors during her trial, "I love to see death in all its forms and phases and left no opportunity to gratify my tastes for such sights. Could I have had my own way, probably I should have done more." Martha was hanged in the Allegheny County jail yard on January 19, 1866, at age 50. The Pittsburgh Press dubbed her the *Arch Murderess* exclaiming: *Pittsburg can claim the unwelcome distinction of having produced one of the most horrifying types of female poisoner that ever darkened the pages of criminal records.*

Martha was not done scaring the people of Pittsburgh. Nor was she done exploring her love for seeing death in its final form even after swinging by her neck in the jail yard.

The midnight after Martha hanged, people in the Fourth Ward of Allegheny City began seeing her ghost. At first, it appeared to just a select few who knew Martha where she had committed the poisonings. Then, as written in the Pittsburgh Daily Post of April 10, 1869: *It is, as if at first, it came reluctantly and under protest to the scene of the deeds that made it so terribly unwelcome, but audacious at length, found a kind of grim delight in spreading a shadowy horror where its tangible horrors of other days were so many and so fell.*

The first, a group of young men chatting on a corner, noted a woman was strolling up from the river's edge. She was hardly distracting as her clothing mirrored any woman strolling the streets. As she passed, with a strange fascination, the men began to note the familiarity the woman had with Martha Grinder—as some had seen her face in the newspapers and another, knew her personally. She passed with eyes downcast and a heavy troubled look. They all became silent, grasping the woman they were seeing was supposed to be dead. Oddly, although a breeze was kicking up from the river, her dress nor the ribbons on it fluctuated with the beat of the wind. The heels of her boots did not clack on the ground, and the soles did not grind on the gritty brick surface of the street. Incredibly, as their mouths dropped, they could see right through her to the brick walls and glass windows of the homes she passed. Then she completely evaporated into the darkness of the walkway.

Others began to see her not long after—a servant girl and a cousin sitting on the employer's steps watched in horror as the woman shuffled past—they too recognized the apparition as Martha Grinder. Curious if this ghost existed, a young man drew his courage one evening and followed the woman working her way past him and then along the street.

When he caught up to her, he stretched out his arm, fingers wiggling—and they went right through, catching only the misty air.

Three Rivers Heritage Trail. *Image: Allie Caulfield.*

Missus Grinder's ghost appeared for several years, then the uproar caused by her ghostly performance seemed to fade away as quickly as the sensation of her murders. But you can walk the path now where passersby saw her ghost along Three Rivers Heritage Trail near the old Hand Street Bridge (now Ninth Street Bridge/Rachel Carson Bridge). Perhaps as you step along the river, you will see Martha Grinder. However, I will highly suggest if she asks you to come in for some soup or to share a cup of tea, you decline.

And just a couple more—

If you like Old Allegheny City ghosts, the ravine of Pleasant Valley offered up a few. On North Charles Street (once Taggart Street), a woman in a wedding gown would race up and down the road searching for her betrothed who died on their wedding night.

Charles Street. *Image: Historic Pittsburgh*

On that same street, a ghostly old-fashioned hearse drawn by two white horses would make a slow and steady pace on the first Monday after a full moon. It carried a little girl's white coffin. She was the first child to die during a smallpox epidemic. Beside the hearse, a little dog ran to be with his young friend.

Finally, there is the old Ridgewood Incline (gone) ghost— a headless man who, on a cold winter's night, fell off the incline and came back to haunt it once a month.

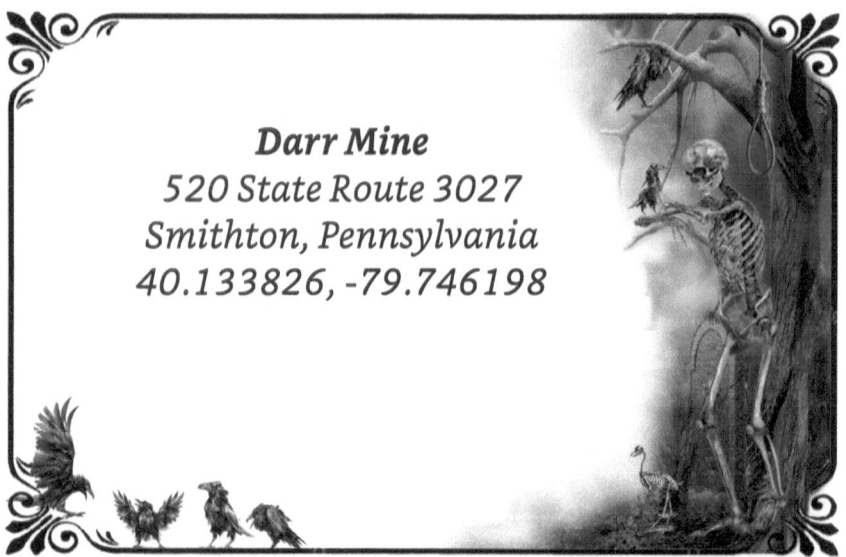

**Darr Mine**
*520 State Route 3027*
*Smithton, Pennsylvania*
*40.133826, -79.746198*

## Explosion at Darr Mine—Ghosts and Miracles

Darr Mine—before its demise in Van Meter, Pennsylvania. The site of a horrific mine disaster, ghosts, and miracles.

Darr Mine was about 30 miles southeast of Pittsburgh in the heart of Pennsylvania's Appalachian coal mining industry. It was an old mine, opened in the 1850s on a hillside above the Youghiogheny River. Nearly 400 miners worked there at any given time, given long hours, where they rarely saw the light of day most of the year.

The workforce was mostly Germans, Greeks, Polish, Austrians, Hungarians, and Italians seeking a better life for their families in the United States. They mainly settled in two towns, one called Van Meter on the same side of the Youghiogheny River as the Darr Mine and another called Jacobs Creek located on the opposite side of the river. Workers from Jacobs Creek took a cable car, the Sky Ferry, across the river to get to work in the morning and then returned the same way in the late evening after a 12 to 14-hour work shift.

The backbreaking work of a coalminer. Miners faced dangerous working conditions, much under complete darkness if not for the open flames of carbide lamps or oil-wick lamps attached to their cloth or canvas caps or helmets—which could be deadly should they run into methane gas deep in the mine. *Image: LOC*

It was hard and dangerous work—cave-ins of rock were not uncommon. Owners of the company did little to protect their miners. The air inside the mine was full of soot, black dust, and deadly methane gas, the latter being a complaint by the miners in Darr Mine, who stated they needed a better ventilation system and more airshafts.

The December of 1907 seemed to bring out the dark colors of the horrors of mining. The Monongah Mine in West Virginia collapsed only weeks earlier due to a series of explosions killing 362 miners. Only days before and on December 1, a blast in the Naomi Mine in Fayette County not far away killed 34 men and closed the mine. Some who had lived came to work at the Darr Mine after. They would have been better without work because something horrid occurred on December 19, 1907. It started as the typical working day for most (it was a short work week, and the mine was closed for the two days before). Two-hundred and forty-nine men and boys would make their way into the mine. Only ten would leave alive.

Darr Mine—the explosion shook the houses for miles.

At 11:30 a.m. that morning, there was a methane gas explosion. At the time, miners wore hats with open flames. A group entered an off-limits area, and those flames caused a spark that ignited the gas. The entire valley shook violently, and for miles away, people felt the earth move. Black smoke bellowed from the gaping mouth of the mine, and then, there was silence. Miles deep within the shaft, 239 men and countless mules lay mangled, burned, and dead.

The layout of the mine—Pittsburgh Dispatch, December 20, 1907

After, eerie voices and the clack of pickaxes striking stone swept up from the hole in the ground, once the mine's entrance. Ghostly stories weaved their way out of the disaster. One came from Ardo Shupe, who lived in Smithton. It was told to him by a young friend who was a trapper boy— young boys whose job was to open the trap door to allow entrance to the mining cars.

15-year-old trapper boy sitting in total darkness waiting for the coal cars. He worked a 10 hour day.

8-10 year-old trapper boy.

Trapper boys had to open the trap door to let the mining cars through. This job had to be done very fast and in a minimal amount of time due to the ventilation and lack of air supply underground—and that the coal car would run him over. One trapper boy at Darr Mine may have been saved by a ghost!

The job was in complete darkness and had to be performed quickly due to the ventilation and lack of air supply underground and, many times, miles deep within the mine. Upon leaving work one evening, the boy, who was probably 12 or 13-years-old, felt a presence walking beside him. Frightened nearly senseless, he ran home at break-neck speed and told his father that he was never going back to the mine again, and it certainly was a ghost that had followed beside him. His father was angry and reprimanded his son, telling him phantoms did not exist, and he certainly would be going back to the mine again the next day, or he would be punished severely. The next two days, the mine was closed. While the boy was not working, he thought hard and decided that perhaps his father was right—it was just his imagination, and no ghosts roamed around.

On the third day, December 19, 1907, the mine reopened, and the boy snatched up his lunch pail and headed off to the mine as usual. However, when he was about to cross the threshold of the mine entrance, an incredible feeling of doubt and terror stopped him. He stood there, then turned on his heels. The young trapper scurried home prepared to deal with a thrashing as long as he did not have to go into that mine again. He was never punished. The Darr Mine explosion killed the young trapper's father and the other miners who worked that day. And a young miner was saved—by a ghost!

The remains of the men and boys who were brought out of the mine by rescuers. Many would never be identified. There were so many, burials were provided by several local cemeteries.

The curious incident with the trapper boy was not the only good that came from something so horrific—some say nothing short of a miracle occurred for countless men who were not there during the explosion. The day of the accident, December 19, was also the Feast of St. Nicholas per the old church calendar—the Orthodox Christian Julian Calendar. A couple of hundred miners were relinquishing a day's wage and threatened with being fired by the mine boss that day. The men refused work to attend church services called Divine Liturgy served at the Jacobs Creek Carpatho-Russian Orthodox Church across the river at Jacobs Creek.

They were not in the mine when the explosion occurred. Instead, the 200 men were in worship—saved by their religious devotion. Their lives were spared. After the tragedy, Carpatho-Russians on both sides of the river dedicated churches to Saint Nicholas in gratitude for the miraculous protection—St. Nicholas Orthodox Church was established in Jacobs Creek and St. Nicholas Byzantine (Greek Catholic) Church in Perryopolis.

**Above**: The memorial for those who died at Darr Mine is just below the main mine portal along The Great Allegheny Passage rail trail system at Mile Marker 107—(40.133826, -79.746198). Just above is the roadway (rear) and on the far side of the road, the mine and some ruins of buildings.
**Below**: The Darr Mine main portal today.

PANORAMIC VIEW OF THE DARR MINE AT JACOBS CREEK, SCENE OF YESTERDAY'S FEARFUL DISASTER

Pittsburgh Post-Gazette December 20, 1907

**Above**: Darr Mine in its heyday. The Darr Mine main portal was sealed in 2015. Seasonally, you can see it from the roadway and there is a small path along the hillside at Van Meter Road (40.133713, -79.746501). Watch for the ruins of an old building. White arrow indicates mine entrance.

Darr Mine was cleaned up by the Pittsburgh Coal Company and reopened as another entrance to Banning Mine #3 in 1910 with safety improvements for the miners. Thirty-five homes were built to house miners and their families in Van Meter. The mine had approximately 350 men and stayed open until 1919.

Ruins of shop.

Mine entrance.

The ruins of the blacksmith shop/machine shop for Darr Mine. Later used as a community building for Van Meter where events like dances were held. (40.133552, -79.746515). If you are facing the building, the mine portal is directly to the right. A small trail leads to the mine.

**Betty Knox Road**
*Along Dunbar Creek*
*Betty Knox Road*
*Dunbar, Pennsylvania 15431*
*39.944499, -79.581229*

## The Legend of Betty and Her Ox

Betty Knox Road where I heard the call of *Betty Knox. Betty Knox.* And then chatter nearby. Was it a ghost?

There is a road in Fayette County called Betty Knox Road. It is named for Betty, who lived in Fayette County by Kentuck and Tharp knobs around the Revolutionary War, from 1775 to 1783. Her mother had died when she was young, and her father raised his only child as any hearty settler would in those old days, training her to farm the land and taking her with him to the mill to grind their grains.

They traveled employing an ox-driven wagon filled with the crops they had harvested to a grist mill in Ferguson Hollow, leaving along a path they had worn with their cart covering the rugged distance. Together, they farmed until Betty's father died when she was hardly out of her teens. She took over the farm and eked out a settler's life without him.

At the time, Isaac Meason, who built Union Furnace in 1791, also owned 6,400 acres of the best coal and iron in Western Pennsylvania that was once the plantation of George Washington's guide, Christopher Gist. Among Meason's other business quests were two local sawmills and a stone grist mill for the grinding of grains. It would be the grist mill that Betty would regularly lead her ox, pulling her wagon full of corn and wheat to grind and garden vegetables to sell in old Union Town. When she went, she did not mingle much with the townspeople, although they saw her and the old ox come and go quite regularly and were curious about this quiet, independent woman.

Tongues wagged after she came to town unescorted on her 28-mile round-trip journey. Among them, townspeople whispered that she had always come alone, for she found a wounded British deserter while the war still played out. She nursed him to health, then harbored the fugitive from the British army that would surely hang him for forsaking his post. So that he would not be caught, he tended the farm while she drove the ox to town by herself.

One day, someone noticed that her routine trips to town had stopped entirely. A search party was sent to look for Betty, but her home was empty, and her animals that had been well-kept were almost starving in the barns and fields. They searched for her everywhere—up and down the roads, along the creeks, in towns, and called out her name— "Betty Knox, Betty Knox!" but to no avail.

That is, until years later, when talk of the woman disappearing and her whereabouts had nearly died down, two boys fishing along a babbling brook found the bones of Betty's old ox tied with a chain to a tree. What had become of Betty? No one may ever know. Some speculate Indians, who were known to harass settlers in the area, might have been the culprits of her vanishing. A cougar or other wild creature may have killed her along the journey to the mill, or thieves may have waylaid her trip.

Some say the curious can still find Betty's spirit standing along that old road, just a bit past the place where Betty Knox Road crosses over Tucker Creek and runs along Dunbar Creek where searchers found the old ox. If you are quiet and park your vehicle by the side of the road, you can hear the mournful cry of the old ox ride the misty air until it fades away with the wind. You can listen to the cry of someone calling her name over and over, "Betty Knox, Betty Knox!"

Betty Knox Road and my jeep which was a happy sight when I visited and where I might have had a close call with a spirit.

But who is calling her name, you might wonder? I may shed some light on the answer because I went for a visit to see if I could see the ghost and hear the calls. Not long after I turned on Betty Knox Road, I parked my jeep and got out. I waited. I listened. The wind was kicking up a bit, and Dunbar Creek was rolling fine after snow and then a thaw. After about ten minutes, I thought I heard laughter and people chattering. It sounded like a church picnic was going on somewhere nearby, but there was not anybody around. I could not quite make out the words. That is when I heard it—*Betty Knox. Betty Knox.* It was deep, almost frantic, and a man's voice calling out loud in the distance like someone holding cupped palms on either side of the lips and hollering for someone who is lost. It stopped. Did I hear it? *Betty Knox. Betty Knox.* I swore I heard it again surging with the water. Then it occurred to me—could it be the babbling clamor of water flowing over the rocks in Dunbar Creek riding on the wind?

There was only one way to find out, I figured, and that was to follow it. *Betty Knox. Betty Knox.* Again, I heard it. It was almost like I would stop and there would be a lull, then it would cry out again. I decided to investigate and walked through the thicket of trees and laurels, followed a little stream, and stopped at the creek. I strolled along the bank for an hour or so, took in a good hike, and picked up some glass worn smooth in the water. *Betty Knox. Betty Knox.*

Hmmm. Now it was across Dunbar Creek. What the heck? I went down a little farther and had to veer off to a deer path and away from the creek to get around a tangled mess of laurel and brush. Not once, but twice. Then I thought I heard the calls just a stone's throw away. I was not sticking with the creek, which is my usual mode of mapping, because, as someone has told me more than once, my sense of direction is so bad, I would get lost in a bucket.

I realized that the calling had stopped, and the chuckle of the creek was far away. No. I heard it again but in a different direction. *Betty Knox. Betty Knox.* It was right about then that I got the heebie-jeebies. And yes, I can find a way out of a bucket when I want to because I made it back to my jeep in record time!

What was the calling? I did not think much of it until I brought up the story to a couple of people two weeks later. And here is how the conversation went—

**Me**: (like I had this happen to me a lot even though I have not): — "So after I heard somebody calling *Betty Knox* the last time, I just decided I imagined it. I hiked a couple more hours and then went back to my jeep and left." (I know, I hustled back. In my defense, I was under pressure in the conversation to not be a scaredy-cat since I occasionally boast that I have been to a lot of haunted places.)

**The person**: "Well, it's a good thing you left."

**Me**: (feeling uneasy again, but trying not to show it): "Um, Why?"

**The other person**, with eyes rolling and looking at me like I have never written a folklore book in my life, answered: "Haven't you ever heard of a calling ghost?"

I shudder to think about it now, but I had not. I was quick to find out that it is a spirit that calls to you or calls your name to lure you to your death. I guess on my trip, I was lucky. Perhaps, Betty and her ox were not.

## Old Irishtown Road
### 110-150 Topper Lane
### Dunbar, PA 15431
### 39.950885, -79.598321

## Ghost Rock

The Ghost Rock—where the spirit of a man carrying a lantern appears.

There is a short gravel road weaving its way into State Gameland 51 outside Dunbar. It is not far from Old Irishtown, where many locals lived and worked in the ore and coal mines. Along this route, wealth dug from deep within the earth's belly would be carried off by rail cars.

There is a massive boulder at the side of the road, and at one time, a worker was killed there by one of the iron ore carts when it derailed. Some nights, passersby can see the man's ghost waving a lantern near the rock, and so, it has been aptly named Ghost Rock.

*Haydentown*
*Georges Township, PA 15478*

## Moll Derry—They Called Her a Witch

Moll Derry was called a witch by some for her skill in healing and an uncanny sense of perception. It has been passed down she came with her husband and fought during the Revolutionary War for the British before deserting and joining the colonists. It is not unlikely. She would not be the only badass musket-slinging woman in the 1700s. Nancy Morgan Hart, above, fought against six armed British soldiers that entered her home and demanded she cook them supper. She fought against them and shot one dead. The rest were hanged when help arrived.

Mary "Moll" and Valentine "Felty" Derry came to America during the Revolutionary War. Felty was a Hessian soldier—a German hired as a mercenary by the British army to fight the colonists in America. He eventually deserted to fight with the Americans under the command of Daniel Morgan's sharpshooters.

After the war, the couple settled on a tract of land at the foot of the mountains in Georges Township, Fayette County, not far from Uniontown. They began to raise a family— seven children in all from 1793 to 1822. Felty became quite renowned for his hunting prowess, so much so that some whispered that he could charm any wild beast into civility before taking it down. Those who lacked hunting skills would see him rubbing a concoction on his clothing and shoes and believe he was using wizardly powers to charm his prey while, he was actually adding scent to his garments to entice bucks toward him. Felty knew how to scout, and he knew how to track. He was proficient with a weapon from his career as a sharpshooter during the war.

The mountains in Georges Township, PA near Haydentown that Moll Derry would call home.

While Felty had a talent for hunting, Moll had a knack for healing. Before modern antidotes, many herbal and natural remedies, along with prayer, were used to cure the sick or injured. Moll was well-traveled. Along her way, she had become proficient with knowing the right invocation to use with the correct treatment culled from the natural world around her. They were a mixture of the cures from the cultures Moll had come into contact with—both in her birth country and her new home. She melded those cultural medicines and practices together to come up with the best treatment—many quite possibly appearing out of the ordinary and strange paths to heal to those around her. But they worked.

Whether providing a smooth, round stone in the pasture near a barn to heal a horse's lame hoof, using willow for pain along with a reading of scripture, or using moss to pack a wound, the relief would be welcome. Yet, there will always be those who are distrustful of anything they believe peculiar, outlandish, or unfamiliar. Perhaps she put a broom by the front door to keep out evil spirits, not an uncommon superstition at the time. Some might see it and take it one step farther, thinking she was parking her mode of transportation on the porch. That aura lent to whispers in the surrounding communities that certain powers were conjured, either good or evil, so many called her a witch.

Many believe she did have special powers. Moll was known to be able to remove hexes and find almost anything lost. This was written in the Juniata Sentinel and Republican from Mifflintown, Pa February 19, 1879, and titled: The Mountain Hunter—*"She was famous, not only in the neighborhood, but in places more remote, as a "Fortune Teller." Young men and maidens and those of a more mature age and wisdom visited her mountain home in the hopes of hearing of something that would help them for either weal or woe.*

*Was anything lost or stolen, whether horse or cow, pocket-book, money, jewels, silver spoons, or any other thing of real or imaginary value, the powers of this celebrated fortune-teller, having the well known name of Moll Derry, were frequently called into requisition. Many and miraculous were the stories treasured in the memory of the oldest inhabitants, and related for fireside entertainment, of her actually telling, without any hint, the article lost, when and where it could be found, and if stolen, the description of the thief, whether male or female. Certain it is, if character be a test of truth, tradition has awarded to Moll Derry the title at least of being a remarkably good guesser. Her invariable dress was a short gown and petticoat, fabricated from the raw material, and from her own hand. Her method of unfolding the future destiny of any of her votaries was done through the simple medium of coffee. The parties seeking their fortunes had to take with them, in addition to money, a certain portion of the article first mentioned. This was prepared in the usual way, care being taken that it should be strong, and that a goodly quantity of the sediment or grounds should adhere to the sides and bottom of the cup. After the liquid had been leisurely sipped, Moll, during the sipping operation, would closely scan the visage of her subject, creating the impression that she was then in search after coming revelations. The cup being placed in the left hand of the seeker, bottom upwards, and the subject required to turn the cup three times, being careful to turn the cup toward the seeker, Moll would then take the cup, and by the grounds that adhered to the sides and bottom, read off the seeker's fortune. It was thought by many that Moll had intimate dealings with the devil. As far as known, she harmed no one, and if she got her money and coffee, she was always contented."*

Moll was born in 1765 and died in 1843. Historians know little of her daily life without the blend of superstitious tales and less of her early years before coming to America. Mystery has and always will surround her.

Walking the trails the legendary Moll Derry may have walked. The land where she lived is mostly private property. But if you'd like to get a feel for her home, you can hike Forbes State Forest or the state gameland: Whitetail Trail Parking Fairchance, PA 15436 (39.808312, -79.693656)

Some have described Moll as being so small she slept in a cradle and then, as a stooped, aged hag with an uncanny reputation of casting spells. Townspeople spoke that if a housewife angered her, she would cast a spell so the bread would refuse to rise. To break the magic, the jinxed housewife would have to heat a horseshoe white-hot, then cool it, and place it above her front door, showing all the neighbors she had tried to deceive ol' Moll and got her just reward.

While she was alive, she cast a spell on three men who had ridiculed her skills, declaring they would be hanged. One was John McFall, who, in a drunken rage, pulled the door of John Chadwick's tavern straight off the hinges to get within the pub, dragged Chadwick outside, and murdered him with a club. McFall was captured and sent to jail. He became the first to be hanged—it was on a Sycamore at what is now the Fayette County Fairground.

The second occurred sometime after 1800. A peddler stopped at a Smithfield tavern to spend the night. Two men, Ned Cassidy and John Updyke, noted the peddler was carrying a large amount of cash on him. They made friends with him and drank at the tavern, then moved on to the White Horse Tavern. As the peddler began to get very drunk, the two men convinced the peddler to head to Haydentown with them a few miles away. It was not an hour later when a bystander witnessed the three traveling along a field with a brushy thicket near John Updyke's home. The next morning, a passerby noted cattle were tearing at the dirt in the scrub. When he checked upon it, he saw blood and a place someone had tied a horse. The tracks of the horse were followed, and a bloody handprint was found on the fence bar in the field.

Authorities never arrested the two men for killing the peddler. Updyke died not long after, and most believed Cassidy had poisoned him to keep him quiet about their ghastly deed. After Updyke's death, Cassidy disappeared to the West and ended up murdering another man. A judge sentenced him to hang, and before he died, he confessed to the peddler's death and stated the two murderers had sunk the body in a mill dam. And what about the third? It seems the third was so distraught at what was to become of him because of the curse, he went off and bought a rope, placed it around his neck, and hung himself!

### White Rocks
**Contact: Forbes State Forest**
**For up-to-date trail info-**
Laughlintown PA 15655
39.829782, -79.710677
### Little White Rock Cemetery
265 Mountain Road
Uniontown, PA 15401
39.836321, -79.732703

## Ode to Polly Williams

White Rocks. Where the legend of Polly Williams begins and ends in a frightful tale. *Image: West Virginia and Regional History Center.*

There was a quilting party on Tuesday, August 14, 1810, at Job Littell's home. He was a local mill-owner whose property was at the foothills of Chestnut Ridge outside Colonel Oliphant's Furnace and not far from Hutchinson Reservoir 2 today. Some of the party worked their way to the gathering on the dirt lane and noticed a young couple, strangers to the community, starting up the hill on a path.

They thought little of it; a thunderstorm was looming on the horizon, and it had caught their full attention. Their own feet were making quick steps because suddenly, the clouds burst rain from the sky.

The air had been sweltering that afternoon after the storm passed. But the children were able to get out to play, and the gathering was in full steam when suddenly, from outside, there was gut-wrenching, high-pitched shriek after shriek rendering the air. Everyone dropped what they were doing and ran out thinking that a snake had bitten a child. But every child whose parents called their names frantically into the air came rushing back unhindered but also claiming to have heard the frantic cries off in the distance. Then sighing in relief and believing it was nothing more than some naughty child feigning terror, they went back to their quilting.

Paths through the laurel forest and the perfect place for collecting blueberries and huckleberries—and finding dead bodies.

It was a warm Saturday, August 18, only four days later, and the perfect kind of morning for picking the tart huckleberries growing along the ridges above Georges Creek less than a mile away. Four children were on this venture—

Susan Hayden, Anne Smiley, and Bess and Hugh Wilson had worked their way along Cave Ridge when one of them noted something white peeking out of the thick, late-spring brush beneath a large outcropping of sandstone called White Rocks. To get a closer look-see, the curious children clambered across the rugged, rock-strewn terrain until they came upon a horrid sight—the broken and lifeless body of a young woman with golden, blood-stained hair and a white dress lying at the foot of the rocks.

Below White Rocks where a young woman's broken body was found by children in 1810.

Nobody knew who the pretty girl of about 17 years of age was and whose corpse lay at the bottom of White Rocks, although it was surely murder. There were huge gashes on her head—three inches long and an inch deep as if someone had struck her before her fall. Beside her head, there lay a rock with blood smeared all over it and hair attached.

Someone found her hat, hair comb, and one slipper high on the rock. Her fingertips were blackened and bruised. Partially down the gap, a laurel had grown from between a cleft of rocks. On her way down, she had desperately reached out to snatch at that laurel branch, and it snapped with her force, for when they found her body, she clutched the stick tightly in her dead fist.

Authorities brought the girl's corpse to the home of Moses Nixon near John Oliphant's whiskey distillery. They laid out the girl, who had deep blue eyes and golden-curled hair, for all to examine. Perhaps in doing so, they would find a family to claim her. Police investigated the death on Sunday, and a jury decided that, indeed, someone had murdered her, but who the killer was, they did not know. It was inevitable that they needed to bury the young woman after a day, and so they did on Monday in the Hayden Cemetery (aka Little White Rock Cemetery).

The graveyard where the murdered girl was buried. A new stone is on the upper end and an older one at the foot.

Then a man from New Salem came forward, claiming the young woman as his niece. The cemetery caretaker exhumed the body, and sure enough, she was identified.

His name was Major Jacob Moss. The dead 18-year-old girl was Mary "Polly" Williams. She had been staying with her uncle and his family doing light housework in exchange for her board. Her mother and father had moved to Steubenville, looking for jobs. The girl was engaged to be married to a local boy. They were soon to be wed, and she did not want to leave with her family.

Major Moss divulged Polly's story—that she had left with a man named Philip Rodgers. The two had planned to marry, and they were heading for Woodbridgetown nearly 16 miles away to complete the ceremony. When the ceremony was complete, the newlyweds had planned on visiting another uncle. Such, the young woman had not been missed when she did not return that day. There had been concerns, though. Short, stout, and pugnacious, 24-year-old Rodgers would hardly be called a catch for sweet and pretty Polly to those who knew him. But he was a smooth-talker and hid behind an amicable demeanor when he wanted to socialize with certain ladies. Rodgers's family was also wealthy, which must have outweighed his substandard character. Still, his parents had resisted the marriage because they felt her family came from a too-humble background.

Rodgers was arrested and tried in court with the following grounds: "being mad and aided by the devil on August 14 1810, with force and arms at the county aforesaid in and upon Mary Williams, in the peace of God and the commonwealth of Pennsylvania, in there and then having feloniously, willfully and of his malice aforethought, did make an assault and that the said Philip Rodgers, a certain stone of no value, which he, the said Philip Rodgers, in both his hands then and there, had and held in and upon the back of the head and side of the face of her, the said Mary Williams, then and there feloniously—"

The spot where Polly's body fell has not changed much since her death.
*Image to left: West Virginia and Regional History Center. WVU*

And today—

It was brought to the jury's attention that Polly had been beaten, then tossed off the cliff. Her fingers were bruised as if someone had taken a stone and, as she clung to the edge, struck her hands until she could no longer hold on. A bloody path from the side showed her fingers and palms had dragged the stone as she fell down the cliff which later, would become a quest for local children to climb to the rocks and search out said bloody fingerprints.

But unbelievable as it might sound, Rodgers was acquitted on the grounds there was not enough evidence. He stated he and Polly had openly fought, and she had walked away and gotten lost. Then she fell off the cliff edge. There were no witnesses to prove him wrong. His family hired the best attorney they could find. It was also quite openly discussed that the jury was threatened to decide in his favor. But the public agreed he was guilty and so made Rodgers's life so miserable staying in the county, he eventually left.

A stone was erected at Polly's grave years later. Over the years, it has been replaced with new. The epitaph reads: *Behold with pity you that pass by. Here does the bones of Polly Williams lie. Who was cut off in her tender bloom. By a vile wretch, her pretended groom.*

Of all the tragedies that render ghosts, shunned lovers, and heartbreaking deaths tend to top the list. Thus, it should be no surprise some have seen Polly Williams's ghost atop White Rocks. She appears not ethereal at all but as bright as the day she stood there over two hundred years ago. She stands there alone, then suddenly whips right to left, thrashed by spectral hands. She turns slightly as if ghostly palms are pushing her backward and begins to fade. Then, she completely disappears.

Standing where Polly fought for her life on White Rocks. But not as close to the edge. Moll Derry, who was from this area during the same era, was reported to have predicted Polly's death.

There is a trail/old road off Hi To Road outside Fairchance to White Rocks, but it passes through private property. The Department of Conservation and Natural Resources (DCNR) Bureau of Forestry manages the area around White Rocks as a part of Forbes State Forest. It will offer a trail and resources to hike to White Rocks on public lands. The site is a habitat for copperheads and timber rattlesnakes that may be sunning themselves on rocks, and the endangered green salamander too. Step lightly because you are on their domain! Oh, and Polly's too.

## Fort Necessity National Battlefield
### National Pike
### Farmington, PA 15437
### 39.815418, -79.588815

## Ghosts of Washington's Only Surrender

The battle at Fort Necessity (depicted in a diorama of the battle in the visitor center) was bloody and was the first steps into the French and Indian Wars. It left behind a few ghosts in its wake.

They both wanted it—the vast territory along the immense Ohio River valley. France and Great Britain would lay claim to the land that included what is today portions of Ohio, Indiana, Kentucky, Pennsylvania, and West Virginia.

Each sent explorations into this vast unknown—the English with Virginians as the Ohio Company and the French that had colonies in Canada and the Louisiana Territory and wanted to maintain the open connection between the two. Then in the 1750s, the French crossed the line in the eyes of the English by building Fort Presque Isle near Lake Erie and Fort Le Boeuf in the Ohio country owned by Virginia.

A young George Washington, a mere 21-years-old, had been sent to Fort LeBeouf in the Ohio Territory as a British emissary in midwinter 1753 and asked the French to leave. They politely refused. Knowing these claims to the territory would continue, Virginia's governor, Robert Dinwiddie, would soon dispatch Washington to build and defend a fort along the Forks of the Ohio River.

*Right: Interior of fort.* Washington built a fort which was not huge at all as you can see in this mirror image reconstructed at Fort Necessity Battlefield Park. During the battle, Washington had 400 men. Obviously, all could not fit in here. The original was burned by the French when they left.

*Left: Exterior of fort.* It also was in a swampy area called Great Meadows that held water through a downpour during the battle. Many died within and around its walls. Listen for voices and ghostly sounds of battle.

As Washington's British soldiers and a group of Mingo warriors arrived in May of 1754, they found French detachments led by Ensign Joseph Coulon de Jumonville in the area. Washington and his men ambushed the French, and in the process of the fight, Jumonville was killed.

Knowing that the French would respond with an attack, Washington hastily built a fort in a place called Great Meadows—Fort Necessity. He was spot-on. On July 3rd, 1754, and in the pouring rain, French soldiers and their Ohio Country Indian allies overpowered Fort Necessity and forced Washington to surrender and abandon the fort. Thirty-one died beneath Washington's command, and three on the French side died. The ripples of the battle would lead outward globally to what is called the Seven Years' War. And it would leave a spirited impact on the land.

A young George Washington retreated with his troops after the surrender at the Battle of Fort Necessity. *Boston Public Library*

There have been reports of supernatural voices—Native Indian, British, and French. The ghostly blare of musket fire rings out in the air, and no reenactors or hunters are around. Visitors have heard footsteps in the visitor center along with indistinct chatter—all remnants of this battleground's violent past.

**Braddock's Grave - Fort Necessity National Battlefield**
National Pike
Farmington, PA 15437
39.832640, -79.601076

## Ghost at Braddock's Grave

Braddock's Monument at Fort Necessity.

Near the Fort Necessity Battlefield is the grave of General Braddock, who was mortally wounded at Braddock's Field in Pittsburgh on his doomed passage to the Forks of the Ohio River to seize French-held Fort Duquesne. He did not die there. Instead, he fled with his retreating soldiers along the great road his men had cut through the wilderness weeks earlier—Braddock's Road.

When he died on July 13, 1755, the men buried him discreetly at Great Meadows. Wagons and horses were allowed to cross over his grave to obscure it as warring Indians were known to dig up graves, desecrate the bodies of those buried, and steal their scalps.

In 1804, workers repairing the roadway found the general's remains. For protection, they were moved to a safe location nearby with the addition of a monument. Over the years, people driving along the road say they see little lights between the roadway and the memorial. Some have even encountered General Braddock's ghost standing at or near the highway or by the monument.

**Long Gone Suspension Bridge
over Jacobs Creek**
*Mount Pleasant Road
Mt Pleasant, PA 15666
40.112512, -79.553373*

## Spirits of Old Iron Bridge

The area where the Old Iron Bridge once stood. Watch as you pass. You might see a ghost.

To the left of this modern bridge, there was once an innovative bridge spanning Jacobs Creek between Connellsville and Mount Pleasant built by James Finley of Uniontown in 1801. It was designed with suspension chains holding a road deck and the first iron suspension bridge in Pennsylvania. The bridge lasted 25 years.

A ghost haunts the area, and talk of a shadowy spirit traversing the roadway here has been around for nearly 200 years. However, no one seems to recollect to whom the ghostly form belongs. There have been a few deaths here tragic enough for a ghostly visit or two. In March of 1912, a 12-year-old newsboy waiting for his evening supply of papers leaned against the rusted railing, and it broke. He plummeted into Jacobs Creek and drowned. If that were not enough to cause a spectral visit occasionally, in 1920, a woman was found dead in the creek. She was clutching a market basket, and it was believed that she strayed off the bridge after dark on a return from the market and fell into the muddy waters below.

**Horseshoe Bend at Rices Landing**
State Route 1010
(Rices Landing Road or Horseshoe Bend Road)
Rices Landing, PA 15357
39.948680, -80.003947

## Stovepipe

Rices Landing circa 1923 along the Monongahela River at the old Lock 6. *Image: Historic Pittsburgh*

In 1755, George Washington and his men found a shallow area of the Monongahela to cross to join forces with Braddock to fight the French and Indians. A little over thirty years later, a man named John Rice would buy this section of land, build a community, and call it Prospect. It would later be named Rices Landing and prosper with stores, liveries, and businesses.

The sharp bend of the hairpin turn where the headless ghost of Stovepipe is conjured up with a calling of his name.

Less than a quarter of a mile from Rices Landing on State Route 1010, a section of steep roadway ends in a hairpin curve. It is called Horseshoe Bend. In the early 1900s, a man drove his carriage along Horseshoe Bend far too fast and lost control of the horse. As he got to the curve, the horse turned to follow the road, but the carriage tipped on to two wheels, then turned over. The man flipped out, and the back wagon wheel sliced his head off. Passersby discovered his body and noted that the wagon wheel so crushed his neck, it looked like a flattened section of stovepipe. His head took a little longer to discover as it had rolled down the embankment on the far side of the road. It was not long after travelers along Horseshoe Bend reported seeing the man's headless ghost lying there when they passed. As the years went by, other folks passing through the area would search for the headless ghost. If they did not see it, they would call out, "Stovepipe! Stovepipe! Stovepipe!" And the spirit would come rambling up from the embankment where he was still searching for his head.

***Rices Landing Jailhouse***
*126 Water Street*
*Rices Landing, PA 15357*
*39.949589, -79.999832*

## *Jailhouse Specter*

The old jailhouse at Rices Landing.

The Rices Landing Jailhouse was built around 1912. As the town and railway system grew, so did the number of vagrants and drunks showing up. It started with one cell, but within a year, another was added—both 8-foot by 8-foot cells with 8- foot ceilings.

Peering through the tunnel at Rices Landing at the place where the old jailhouse was moved while standing near the place that it once stood.

The jailhouse was used until 1940, and food was provided to those within by local restaurants. It used to sit just inside the Pumpkin Run Park by the tunnel but was removed due to erosion on the steep incline leading to the creek beneath it. The tiny building was heated with natural gas, which once malfunctioned (the gas shut off and when it turned back on, it did not relight), and a man was asphyxiated inside. If you go for a visit, tip your head toward the door. Listen. You might hear chit-chat inside. Or scratching by whatever is in there that wants outside!

*Greene River Trail:*
*Rices Landing Trailhead*
*Rices Landing, PA 15357*
*Parking:*
*39.951970, -80.004240*

## The Haunting of Greene River Trail

The Greene River Trail is a hike/bike trail running along the Monongahela and through Rices Landing. Those on the path have reported seeing shadowy figures that appear very tall and slender. They seem to be quite curious about the passerby while they lurk in the darkness—watching, watching, watching.

**Pumpkin Run Park**
*Off Main Street*
*Rices Landing, PA 15357*
*39.949382, -80.000480*
*Open: Memorial Day through Labor*
*Day from 9:00 a.m. to dusk*
*(Always check park for seasonal*
*changes in dates and times)*

## Old Ruins with Old Ghosts

Leftovers of old industry along Pumpkin Run.

At Rices Landing, there is a park—Pumpkin Run Park that embraces ruins of some early industries in the region, including an old quarry and the John Hughes Grist Mill. If you walk under the tunnel off Main Street and follow the gravel road back, you will eventually come to a bridge. After crossing the bridge, old stones mark the ruins. Picnickers and hikers have heard eerie flute music issuing from the quarry and mill, believed to be a long-dead employee reliving a relished break from work.

***Intersection of
Bethel Ridge Road and
Shades of Death Road***
*Avella, PA 15312
40.314967, -80.490149*
*To*
***Intersection of
Shades of Death Road and
Campbell Drive***
*Avella, PA 15312
40.306545, -80.465302*

## Shades of Death

Shades of Death Road.

In the early days, travelers named the gloomy, dark road connecting Bethel Ridge Road and Campbell Drive *Shades of Death* because the trees fit so tightly together that the canopy blocked out the sky even during the day. Over time, the timbering of hemlocks has eliminated some of that darkness. But then, as now, it has been a source of many ghostly tales.

Some people say that a Pittsburgh-Steubenville stagecoach was waylaid by robbers and taken to this dreary road. The thieves stole all the passengers' money before murdering them along with the driver. The long-dead travelers make wispy trails through the trees along the roadside, leering at the living and pondering ways they can wreak out justice on them as they could not avenge their deaths to the actual murderers.

Then, there are claims that several dead miners from the Cliftonville Riot were buried in unmarked graves by their fleeing comrades in the deep woods around the road. On July 17, 1922, and a muggy Monday morning, 500 union miners marched along a ridge above Cliftonville to stop nonunion workers from mining.

The headhouse and conveyer burning after the Cliftonville Riot. Some conclude the sounds seeping from the woods and the dark shadows are ghosts of miners long-gone from that battle. *Image: West Virginia and Regional History Center*

At about 5:15 a.m., and just as the unwitting nonunion miners started for work, the army of union men burst through the woods. The men charged downward into the town and by the tipple. During an ensuing battle that lasted until around 7:00 a.m., fighters killed Brooke County Sheriff H.H. Duval and at least 13 miners.

By then, the union-working wounded and dying had been snatched up and disappeared into the surrounding woodland, including the thick-treed area a couple of miles away around Shades of Death Road. Many believe that the bloodcurdling screams, groaning, and growling are the souls of the dead rioters buried there—dropped quickly so their living cohorts could escape while being ensued.

If you dare to take Shades of Death Road, watch for dark things slithering in the woods. Just remember, though, these mysterious beasts of darkness are protected by private property so do not get out and chase them into their lairs.

## St. Lawrence Catholic Church— Statue of Mary
3223 Churchill Road
Edinburg, PA 16116
41.015305, -80.492398

### Finding Safe Passage to Zombie Land

If her hands are folded, stay away from Zombie Land!

If you dare to enter Zombie Land north of Hillsville, let the ivory statue of the Virgin Mary advise you if it is safe. If her arms are open and her palms extended, you can enter safely. But if her hands are folded, beware—danger lies ahead in this area full of haunts, paranormal activity, and zombie people who live under a bridge.

## St. Lawrence Cemetery
### Churchill Road/E River Road
### Edinburg, PA 16116
### 41.015795, -80.491738

### *Glowing Grave*

St. Lawrence Cemetery—A grave glows here.

The first step along your journey entering Zombie Land is a drive-by of the St. Lawrence Cemetery just past the church. While you pass, watch for the glowing tombstone in the cemetery. The area is also home to the *Green Man*, a handyman electrocuted while working, whose fluorescent body glows as he roams the roads along the route.

**Hilltown Bridge**
*E River Road*
*Edinburg, PA 16116*
*41.019623, -80.489157*

## Spectral Lights, Hellhounds, Killing Fields, and All Things Wicked

Sitting on Hilltown Bridge and staring out at the fields—The Killing Fields, that is. It is full of all sorts of creepy things including baying hellhounds.

If you keep driving about 1/3 mile, you will cross the Hilltown Bridge over the Mahoning River. Over the years, it has changed and upgraded from the original rickety bridge that finally succumbed to floods and age. Witnesses have seen strange lights appear beneath it and in the field beyond, hellhounds and other things wicked lurk.

**Bridge over Coffee Run**
*Skyhill Road over Coffee Run*
*Pennsylvania 16116*
*41.043148, -80.491658*

## Graffiti Bridge

This bridge has replaced the old Graffiti Bridge, but it inherited its creepy legend— That said, I hoped my name was not on it—

If you make a left after Hilltown Bridge, then left on Skyhill Road, you will come to another bridge. People call it by many names, including Frankenstein Bridge, Puerto Rican Bridge, and Graffiti Bridge. It is a place where a young man committed suicide. If you see your name written on the bridge, the murderous people (zombies) living beneath the bridge will climb up the sides, snatch you up, and drag you kicking and screaming back into their dark abode.

**Zombie Land Torch**
*New Castle Struthers Road*
*Pulaski, PA 16143*
*41.042941, -80.492345*

## The Summoning Torch

The zombie summoning torch.

The final quest on your Zombie Land tour is just off Skyhill Road, about 200 feet west of the bridge. It is the Zombie Land Eternal Flame or Torch. If lit, the zombies are summoned and will appear for your grand finale. This iron pipe is a vent from an old oil and natural gas field. Do not light it lest you want to take the chance of also beckoning more than just zombies—the county coroner, for example, or death.

### *Coverts Crossing Bridge*
*Brewster/Covert Road*
*New Castle, PA 16102*
*40.996350, -80.414872*

## *Bridge of Many Ghosts*

The bridge then.

The bridge now.

The Mahoning River was always a dangerous place to cross either via foot or horseback. Coverts Crossing Bridge was a welcome sight opened for service around 1887. It was a one-lane bridge with wooden planks for many years before it was paved. When it was paved, the development had to stop for an archeological dig—workers found many Indian artifacts beneath. The bridge became the foundation for many ghost stories—from a railroad worker who fell off the side, a young girl murdered on prom night, and a couple who drove off the side in their horse and buggy. If you parked near the bridge and turned off the lights in its early years, an apparition would appear.

**Hell's Hollow**
**Hells Run to Spirit Falls**
**McConnells Mill State Park**
*1436 Shaffer Road*
*Portersville, PA 16051*
*40.931342, -80.239742*

## Legend of Harthegig

Hell's Run along Hell's Hollow Trail.

Around two miles from Mercer, there is a lone hollow that was once a part of the hunting grounds of Indians. As the settlers began to move into this fertile land in the late 1700s, small cabins dotted the landscape, and both settlers and Indians tolerated each other as best they could.

In the late 1790s, the Pews were one of those families living along a ravine overlooking a dark and narrow gully near what is now Old Sharon Road. Frequently friendly Indians would stop in for a visit. Still, there was one known as Harthegig, a huge beast of a man who was quite surly and had a reputation as being a drunk. He was said to be broad-shouldered and ugly, and the Pew children tried to stay far away from him on his visits because he would tweak an ear or pinch an arm or find some way to bully them.

Samuel Pew was the eldest son of the Pew children. When he was just a young boy, he was sitting on a log by the fire warming himself when Harthegig and two other Indians were visiting. Harthegig suddenly jumped up, grabbed the boy by the hair, and exclaimed: "I will scalp you!" It so terrified those in the home, including a neighbor James Jeffers who greatly disliked Harthegig, that they all sprang quickly to their feet and disarmed the man of his weapons.

The next morning, Samuel was playing near the home, and James Jeffers passed by asking the boy if he had seen Harthegig. He had. Samuel pointed to the direction of a path the Indian had traveled that morning. Jeffers then disappeared up the same way.

Harthegig was never seen alive after that day. It was something of a mystery until nine years later, after heavy rainfall, someone discovered a huge skeleton sticking out of the mud not far away from the Pew home and along a creek. It was that of the missing Indian. People in the community began to whisper that they had, for many years, heard strange moans and groans issuing from that very hollow Harthegig's corpse was found. They dubbed it Hell's Hollow, and the creek flowing through it, Hells Run.

There is a waterfall along a trail fed by that same creek where the murderer secreted the dead man's body. It is called Spirit Falls or Hell's Hollow Falls. People even today say they hear Harthegig's dying moans and groans ride from his lonely grave along the water's path to the falls, and as they run through the rocks to be dumped at the bottom, they are released as gruesome shrieks into the air.

Hell's Hollow Falls.

***Crow Rock Massacre Site***
*Crow Rock Road*
*Wind Ridge, PA 15380*
*39.927666, -80.505720*

## Crow Rock Massacre

Where 4 sisters were passing the time along the way to neighbors in 1791. *And* where 3 men were lurking behind a rock just above the creek, watching them and planning an attack.

It was the warm Sunday morning of May 1, 1791, when four daughters of Jacob Crow, a local miller, left for a walk along Dunkard Fork of Wheeling Creek—Christina (age—7), Susanna (about age—18-19), Catherine (age—6-7), and the eldest who was married with a child, Elisabeth (age—20).

It was a beautiful day, and although there was always fear that unfriendly Indians could be around, it had been quiet thus far, and the early spring day invited them outside and a little farther from home.

They had opted to visit an elderly neighbor who lived in Crabapple Hollow to feel the sunshine on their cheeks and perhaps, pick a few flowers along the way. About a mile into their journey along the shallow creek meandering past their home and their father's mill—Dunkard Fork of Wheeling Creek—they lingered near the water's edge to poke at the stones at the ford they would cross.

Above: the creek where the girls were walking.

Left: The Crow homestead (top left) and grist mill (center). Below the mill is where the attack occurred.

A brother, 21-year-old Michael, passed them with a horse that had strayed out of the pasture and to Wharton Run. It was acting uneasy, and the young man had to hold the reins hard to keep it still. He tried to talk 7-year-old Christina into riding with him, but she refused.

Michael finally rode off, and no sooner than he did, two Indians slipped up from behind a rock ledge. Along with the Indians was another man who was white but who dressed in Indian clothing. While one Indian went to make sure Michael did not return, the other two men snatched up the sisters and marched them up the hillside. As they did, the girls began to converse in their father's native tongue, German, planning for an escape. Angered, the men quieted them quickly, and Elisabeth told her sisters to pray. The men set them on a log, plying them for information about the location of settler homes.

The attackers hid behind this rock, watching the girls walk the creek, below and right.

Upon the return of the second Indian, there was a debate should the girls be murdered or taken into captivity. They decided to kill them, and the men began their attack on the girls, forcing them to clasp each other's hands together.

Each man grabbed the hands of one girl to restrain them, then used their free hand to club them with their ax or musket.

Susanna was hit with a tomahawk and killed. One of the girls was stunned by the first strike and, being older and stronger, began to struggle with her captor. During the melee, Christina was able to slip from her captor's grasp and started to run up an embankment. She was overwhelmed with a hit of the muzzle of his gun to her head. However, when the man left her for dead, she was able to spring to her feet. Christina recounted the ordeal later: "Began to tomahawk one of my sisters-Susan by name. Susan dodged her head to one side, the tomahawk taking effect in her neck, cutting the jugular vein, the blood gushing out a yard's length. The Indian who held her hand jumped back to avoid the blood. The other Indian then began the work of death on my sister Elizabeth, and a third on Katie."

Christina was able to run away and warn her family of the tragedy. She described her flight like this: "I gave a sudden jerk and got loose from the one that held me and ran with all speed, taking up a steep bank, but just as I caught hold of a bush to help myself up, the Indian fired, and the ball passed through the clump of hair on my head, slightly breaking the skin. I gained the top in safety, the Indian taking round in order to meet me as I would strike the path that led homeward. But I ran right from home and hid myself in the bushes near the top of the hill. Presently I saw an Indian passing along the hill below me; I lay still until he was out of sight; I then made for home."

A search party returned for the girls the next day. Michael was among them. Two of the girls were already dead. The third, Elisabeth, had managed to drag herself to the banks of the shallow creek. As Michael kneeled next to her, she said, "Michael, why didn't you come sooner?"

She would die three days later, on May 4, 1791. The family buried the three girls near each other in graves.

Crow Rock.

Monument and Crow Rock just beyond.

The area is haunted. Those nearby have heard hoofbeats pounding the ground, noted dark figures lurking in the shadows, and some even have their hair pulled. The most compelling story is that of a man who, while driving along the road, saw a full-body apparition of an Indian.

### Hill View Manor
*2801 Hill View Manor Drive*
*New Castle, PA 16101*
*40.963269, -80.300735*
*This is on private property, but*
*offers guided tours and ghost hunts.*

## The Haunting of Hill View Manor

The Hill View Manor—appears quite ominous on the hill as you drive up the lane.

The Lawrence County Home for the Aged—Hill View Manor opened its doors outside New Castle in 1926 as a care facility for the aged, homeless, and disabled. It featured a central section and east and west wing on either side of the primary main building. Most of the residents were adults, but there were occasional children taken in. It continued in operation into the 1960s.

Along its way, the Hill View Manor has picked up more than a few ghosts—one unique character is the spirit of Eli, who was a part-time resident when the building was a poor farm. A recovering alcoholic, he would sometimes relapse. After finding a way to town to buy some booze, Eli would make his way back to the poorhouse and steal away to some dark corner to drink because the administration forbade alcohol of any kind in the home. One morning after drinking the night away, he settled down at the front doors and passed out. Other boarders found him and knew there might be repercussions if their buddy was found dead drunk at the entrance where anyone passing the roadway could see him. He might end up in a jail cell instead of a poorhouse bedroom. They secreted him to the boiler room to sober up—but he never did. Eli died there, oblivious to his mates' heroic efforts to protect him.

It is the dank, dark boiler room that offers a ghostly presence of Eli. He tends to pick on women, as many have reported getting pinched or having their hair tugged! But Eli is undoubtedly not the only ghost at the building. A boy of about seven named Jeffrey also roams the building. Witnesses have seen shadow figures wandering the hallways along with wispy clouds that waft through the wings, leaving a chill in the air. There have even been faces seen peering out the windows!

Watch for ghostly faces in the windows!

**Pennsylvania Soldiers'
and Sailors' Home—Fort Presque Isle
(Blockhouse)**
*Ask permission here to visit blockhouse.*
*560 E 3rd Street*
*Erie, PA 16507*
*42.138576, -80.073104*
**Blockhouse:**
*42.140183, -80.074387*

## Mad Anthony Wayne's Ghost

The blockhouse in Erie where General Wayne died and where he is said to begin his ghostly travel searching for his bones.

He was known as Blacksnake by the Native Indians because of his fighting technique of sitting back patiently and waiting for the precise moment to strike. But from the soldiers he led during the American Revolutionary War, he earned another nickname for his ferocious and reckless actions on the battlefield—and from an angered spy named Jemmy the Rover.

Jemmy was placed in jail in 1781 for disorderly conduct. To get out of his imprisonment, the spy tried to persuade the jailers to release him as he was friends with Wayne. When hearing of this claim, Wayne said the man would spend out his time in jail, and if he heard anything about enticing the jailers again, he would "order 29 lashes, well laid on." Which in turn, Jemmy the Rover replied: "Anthony is mad. He must be mad, or he would help me. Mad Anthony, that's what he is. Mad Anthony Wayne!" Such, the nickname "Mad" Anthony Wayne stuck.

In the 1791 Northwest Indian War, Wayne was a large part of the win at the Battle of Fallen Timbers and the resulting removal of American Indian claims to Ohio. He would accept their surrender, and not long after—December 15, 1796, he was seized by an attack of gout that ended up as an infection in his stomach and died at Fort Presque Isle.

In 1809, one of Wayne's sons, Isaac, traveled to Erie to exhume his father's remains to be properly buried at the family plot in Radnor. When the body was unburied, the mummified remains had not decayed enough for an easy trip back to the cemetery. Isaac obtained a large kettle and boiled his father's carcass to nothing but bones small enough to carry in a sack. Along the way, the road (which is U.S. 322) was incredibly bumpy. Some bones were jarred out of the bag and lost along the road, never to be found. Now, some have seen Wayne's ghost. He starts along the same route as his son's travels from the blockhouse and Route 322, forever searching for the lost bones along the way.

**Presque Isle State Park**
*301 Peninsula Drive*
*Erie, PA 16505*
*42.159373, -80.115101*

## Presque Isle Storm Hag

*Presque Isle—Is the oncoming storm held at bay by the Storm Hag? Perhaps she is waiting for unwary boaters to head toward its shores and instead, they will slip into her greedy grasp partway there.*

Presque Isle State Park is a sandy peninsula arching into Lake Erie near Erie. Lake Erie is prone to erratic waves, shifting sandbars, and wild, unpredictable storms. Its treacherous, shallow depths harbor many shipwrecks up and down the coast—an estimated 500 to 3000 ships with their crews dragged down to a watery grave.

Early explorers along the 76 miles of Pennsylvania's shorelines used this peninsula's eastern bay as a windbreak to beach boats during the many volatile storms. Not all those who sought its shelter made it out intact. The Lake Erie Quadrangle—a stretch of 2,500 square miles embracing an expansive shipwreck graveyard holds more wrecks than the Bermuda Triangle. Presque Isle is amid its epicenter.

There is an ancient legend that explains the number of wrecks around Presque Isle. There is a Storm Hag who lives near the peninsula at the bottom of Lake Erie. She is ghastly with green, pasty skin, a pointed chin, and green locks of hair. Her arms are long and her nails sharp. Her eyes are yellow, and her green teeth are sharply pointed like a shark. She emerges once in a while to feed upon those unfortunate sailors who come close to her lair. Before she attacks, she sings an enticing song that flows across the water. Then she calls up a ferocious storm to sink the boat and snatch up her meal. Sometimes she creeps to the land and hides in the trees waiting for little children to wander off from parents so she can stretch out her long arms and drag them to the water and drown them.

A traditional story of the Storm Hag's ruthlessness and Lake Erie's unpredictable squalls centers around a ship caught in a storm on Lake Erie in 1782. Seeing the black clouds rise on the horizon, the captain tried desperately to steer his ship toward Presque Isle's protective peninsula. To get to safety, he had to navigate past a dangerously shallow area before the storm hit, where many boats before him had gone down, trying with the same desperation to get to the shelter of the small bay. He did not make it and watched just short of the treacherous path while the waves beat his boat viciously side to side. He dared not take the risk.

As sweat dribbled down his forehead and his men stared at him with frightened, knowing eyes, doom pass over him.

The calm between the storm—where it seems so safe—but it's not. Especially on Lake Erie with its shallow waters.

In each gaze, he saw the grieving eyes of each mother and wife that he had let down by waiting too long. He would cause the ruin of his crew and the source of many a mourning mother and widowed wife. Suddenly, the storm stopped, and the clouds slipped away to moonlight shining off the calm waters. The sailors sighed, and the captain plotted a course through the shallows.

It was halfway through the dangerous shallows that they heard the soft song slipping through the breeze—the deep lulling wail a hearty wind makes passing through a nearly-closed window. *Come, lads, come. Tis safe, it is.* The men froze in horror as the moonlight dribbled away to darkness, and a foamy fog crept along with the clouds lurking across the sky. *The Siren. The Storm Hag.* She bestowed her fury on the ship in one bolt of lightning and a rousing smash of thunder. She burst from her lair in the bowels of the lake and attacked with the storm relentlessly until the boat vanished with its crew in the black depths.

*Those with a keen eye walking Presque Isle's shores note tiny white crystals lying amidst the sand. It is passed down that the crystals were made from the tears of the wives and mothers of sailors lured to their death by the Storm Hag after she released her fury and dragged the ship and crew into the dark waters below. When tucked into the palm, these crystals were used as charms to ward off the Hag and her wicked manipulation of the storms for her gain. Each unleashed a powerful rage from widows and mothers aimed at the Hag stealing the lives of loved ones.*

***Graveyard Pond Trail***
*Presque Isle State Park*
*Thompson Drive*
*42.154724, -80.092714*

## Graveyard Pond

Graveyard Pond, where dead men walk.

A legend goes back to the War of 1812 when Commodore Perry rested his ships in Misery Bay during a bitterly cold winter. Several men died, and their shipmates buried them in the shallow depths of what is called Graveyard Pond. Park visitors have seen their ghosts trudging along the water's edge in raggedy, torn clothing.

# Citations

**Blue Mist Road/Lovers Graves:**
—www.trytoscare.me/legend/blue-mist-road-pittsburgh-pa/
—Pittsburgh Post Gazette October 30, 1994 Folklore of Road Known by Locals
—Pittsburgh Post Gazette VoicesNorth October 30, 1994 Goulish Folklore breeds Legend of Blue Mist Ghost
—https://sites.rootsweb.com/~njm1/03CrossRoads.htm

**Betty and her Ox:**
—The Daily CourierAug 19, 1974
—The Daily Courier Aug 9, 1919_
—The Morning Herald Wed Feb 25,1925
—The_Pittsburgh Press Jun 3,1923

**Ghost Rock:**
—http://booksadventuresandlife.blogspot.com/2011/08/searching-for-haunted-rock-of-irishtown.html
—Ghosts, Banshees and Witches. (n.d.). Retrieved from http://www.histbuffer.com/2015/10/ghosts-banshees-and-witches.html
—Historic Map Works LLC. (n.d.). Historic Map Works, Residential Genealogy ™. Retrieved from www.historicmapworks.com/Overlay/?m=160136&c=US&lat=39.950885&lng=-79.598321
—Searching for the "Haunted Rock of Irishtown". (2011, August 17). booksadventuresandlife.blogspot.com/2011/08/searching-for-haunted-rock-of-irishtown.html

**13 Bends:**
—Kapolka, B. (2016, May 6). 13 Bends : Pittsburgh, PA. Retrieved from https://www.trytoscare.me/legend/13-bends-pittsburgh-pa-2/
—"Haunted" Places in and around Pittsburgh. (2016, April 9). Retrieved from https://sites.psu.edu/mkzpassion/2016/04/09/haunted-places-in-and-around-pittsburgh/

**Darr Mine:**
—Explore more: https://www.wqed.org/ride
—Washlaski, Raymond. DARR MINE. History of the Darr Mine, Van Meter, Rostraver Twp., Westmoreland Co., Pennsylvania, U.S.A. "A forgotten Mine Patch Town." "The Worst Mine Disaster in Pennsylvania." https://tinyurl.com/Darr-Mine
—200 to 300 DEAD IN DARR MINE. (1907, December 20). The Morning Herald [Uniontown, PA].
—The Darr Mine Disaster | WQED. (n.d.). Retrieved from https://www.wqed.org/tv/watch/experience/darr-mine-disaster-0
—Darr Mine Explosion. (n.d.). Retrieved from https://usminedisasters.miningquiz.com/saxsewell/darr.htm
—Haunted Pittsburgh LLC. (n.d.). Retrieved from https://www.facebook.com/PghGhostTour/posts/darr-mine-disaster-worst-ever-in-pennsylvania-and-the-ghost-in-the-mineat-1130-a/10155050764529072/
—Love, Gilbert Did a Ghost Save a Boy's Life at Darr Mine?. (1979, December 31). The Pittsburgh Press.
—Mine Explosion Entombs 250 Men. (1907, December 20). New York Times [New York, NY].
—Remembering the Darr Mine Disaster: the American Hungarian Federation. (n.d.). Retrieved from http://—

www.americanhungarianfederation.org/news_darrmine_victims.htm
—Searching Smithton, PA. (n.d.). Retrieved from http://www.histbuffer.com/2015/05/searching-smithton-pa.html
—Thread by @ErikLoomis: "This Day in Labor History: December 19, 1907. The Darr Mine near Smithton, Pennsylvania, caught fire and exploded. 239 people died, many of [?]". (n.d.). Retrieved from https://threadreaderapp.com/thread/1075497987604918273.html
—WRECKED MINE GIVES UP SIX MANGLED BODIES. .. (n.d.). The Pittsburgh Press at Newspapers.com 20 Dec 1907, Page 1 - [Pittsburgh, Pennsylvania].

**Dead Man's Hollow:**
—Pittsburgh Post-Gazette Pittsburgh, Pennsylvania Thursday, April 06, 2000 - Page 117
P—ittsburgh Daily Post Pittsburgh, Pennsylvania Wednesday, August 03, 1881 - Page 4 DEAD MAN'S HOLLOW
—Pittsburgh Daily Post Pittsburgh, Pennsylvania Friday, August 05, 1881 – Page 4
—The Valley Sentinel Carlisle, Pennsylvania Friday, August 12, 1881 - Page 4
—Pittsburgh Post-Gazette Pittsburgh, Pennsylvania Friday, May 26, 1944 - Page 13
—The Pittsburgh Press Pittsburgh, Pennsylvania Thursday, August 08, 1907 - Page 1
—The Pittsburgh Press Pittsburgh, Pennsylvania Friday, December 01, 1916 - Page 6
—The Somerset Herald Somerset, Pennsylvania Wednesday, March 14, 1883 - Page 2
—https://alleghenylandtrust.org/wp-content/uploads/2016/12/1-Dead-Mans-Hollow-Management-Plan-Final.compressed-1.pdf
—The Pittsburgh Press Pittsburgh, Pa December 01, 1916 - Page 6 INTERPRETER'S BODY FOUND IN CREEK
—Dead Man's Hollow - Popular Pittsburgh. https://popularpittsburgh.com/dead-mans-hollow/

**Dravo Cemetery:**
—Ghost Stories Haunt Spots on Yough River Trail. (2001, October 31). Pittsburgh Post-Gazette (Pittsburgh, Pennsylvania).
—Mary Ravasio, Tri-State Sports & News Service. (n.d.). Tales of unexplained sights and sounds echo along Youghiogheny River Trail. Post Gazette [Pittsburgh, PA].
—White, T. (2014). Supernatural Lore of Pennsylvania: Ghosts, Monsters and Miracles. Charleston, SC: Arcadia Publishing.
—White, Tom. (2002, October 22). Ghost sightings park of local legend. Pittsburgh Post-Gazette (Pittsburgh, Pennsylvania).
—Gresham, John. Biographical and Historical Cyclopedia of Westmoreland County, Pennsylvania Page 618

**Montour Trail:**
—Smith, T. (2012, October 31). Do you believe? Retrieved from https://patch.com/pennsylvania/canon-mcmillan/bp--do-you-believe

—Tunnels and Bridges of the Montour. (n.d.). Retrieved from https://www.montourrr.com/Bridges/Bridges.html
—Pittsburgh Post-Gazette Pittsburgh, Pennsylvania Friday, July 05, 1912 - Page 2
—Pittsburgh Daily Post Pittsburgh, Pennsylvania Sunday, July 07, 1912 - Page 5

**Green Man Tunnel:**
—23 Oct 2002, Page 55 - Pittsburgh Post-Gazette Let's Talk About the Green Man. (n.d.).
—Doctors Marvel that Boy Lives. (n.d.). The Daily Times - Aug 4, 1919.
—Lascoli. (2016, March 2). Green Man Tunnel. Retrieved from — https://maps.roadtrippers.com/us/south-park-township-pa/points-of-interest/green-man-tunnel
—Peters Creek Railroad History. (n.d.). Retrieved from https://phms.peterscreek.org/RailroadHistory1.html

**Roamin' Rosie:**
—Best Pittsburgh Haunts. (2010, November 10). Retrieved from https://pittsburgh.cbslocal.com/top-lists/best-pittsburgh-haunts/
—Southwestern Pennsylvania Guide. (2020, February 8). Retrieved from https://www.swpenna.com/haunted-places-in-pittsburgh/
—threerivershauntsandhistory9 - hauntsandhistory. (n.d.). Retrieved from https://sites.google.com/site/hauntsandhistory/threerivershauntsandhistory4

**Braddock's Field:**
—Retrieved from The Miriam and Ira D. Wallach Division of Art, Prints and Photographs: Print Collection, The New York Public Library. (1775 - 1890). Fall of Braddock http://digitalcollections.nypl.org/items/510d47da-2e75-a3d9-e040-e00a18064a99
—Braddock's Road of Pennsylvania & Maryland – Legends of America. (n.d.). Retrieved from https://www.legendsofamerica.com/braddocks-road/
—Okonowicz, E. (2007). Haunted Maryland: Ghosts and Strange Phenomena of the Old Line State. Stackpole Books.
—WALKING WITH GHOSTS OF THE FRENCH-INDIAN WAR. (2005, July 10). The Baltimore Sun at Newspapers.com [Baltimore Md].
—Whetzel, Dan. (n.d.). Where is General Braddock's Gold? Retrieved from http://www.mountaindiscoveries.com/images/ss2018/stories/17%20Gen%20Braddock.pd
—25 Sep 2001, Page 30 - Pittsburgh Post-Gazette Let's Talk About Braddock's Gold

**Edgar Thomson/Hamburg Road:**
—Lamb, G. H. (1917). The Unwritten History of Braddock's Field. Pittsburgh, Nicholson printing co., Australia.
—The town prosperity killed: Few traces remain of Port Perry. (2004, January 21). Retrieved from https://www.post-gazette.com/local/south/2004/01/21/The-town-prosperity-killed-Few-traces-remain-of-Port-Perry/stories/200401210124

—The Pittsburgh Press Mar 21,1967 Braddock Steels Itself to Ghost

—Pittsburgh Post Gazette Nov 6, 1980 Eerie: The Haunting of Edgar Thomson Works

—PORT PERRY AND TURTLE CREEK - Pghbridges.com. http://pghbridges.com/articles/places/portperry_unwritten.htm

**Southside Ghosts:**

—How 65 Pittsburgh Neighborhoods Got Their Names. (2015, July 29). Retrieved from https://www.mentalfloss.com/article/65575/how-65-pittsburgh-neighborhoods-got-their-names

—Southside Ghosts. (1889, September 8). Pittsburgh Dispatch.

**Ghost of Two Shop:**

—Swetnam, George. (n.d.). The Ghost of Two Shop. The Pittsburgh Press. September 6, 1970.

—White, Thomas. (n.d.). Catholic Ghost Stories Of Western Pennsylvania - A Ghost in the Mill. Retrieved from https://dsc.duq.edu/cgi/viewcontent.cgi?article=1158&context=gf

**Slag Pile Annie:**

—Retrieved from https://www.arcgis.com/apps/View/index.html?appid=63f24d1466f24695bf9dfc5bf6828126

—The Spirits of the Steel Mills. (2019, November 1). Retrieved from https://popularpittsburgh.com/spirits-of-the-steel-mills/

**Martha Grinder:**

—"The American Borgia: Execution of Martha Grinder," New York Times, January 20, 1866, p. 8.

—The Grinder poisoning case: the trial of Martha Grinder, for the murder of Mrs. Mary Caroline Carothers, on the 1st of August, 1865 : being a full and complete history of this important case. Published by John P. Hunt & Co., 1865

—Pittsburgh Daily Post April 10, 1869 The Unrest of Missus Grinder

—4th Ward, Allegheny City. (n.d.). Retrieved from https://historicpittsburgh.org/islandora/object/pitt%3A1872p082/viewer

—Retrieved from https://www.arcgis.com/apps/View/index.html?appid=63f24d1466f24695bf9dfc5bf6828126

—Google Maps. (n.d.). Retrieved from https://www.google.com/maps/dir/40.450891,+-79.995551+/40.44785,-80.000055/@40.4471263,-80.0031194,18z/data=!4m7!4m6!1m3!2m2!1d-79.995551!2d40.450891!1m0!3e2

—Lofquist, Bill. (n.d.). State Killings in the Steel City: The History of the Death Penalty in Pittsburgh. Retrieved from https://state-killings-in-the-steel-city.org/2018/02/15/martha-grinder/

—Sketch of the Life of Mrs. Grinder Is She a Professional Poisoner? (1865, September 3). Retrieved from https://www.nytimes.com/1865/09/03/archives/sketch-of-the-life-of-mrs-grinder-is-she-a-professional-poisoner.html

—Three Rivers Heritage Trail. (2019, March 21). Retrieved from https://friendsoftheriverfront.org/three-rivers-heritage-trail/

—Top 10 Dreadful Accounts Of Women Condemned To The Gallows. https://listverse.com/2017/02/13/top-10-dreadful-accounts-of-women-condemned-to-the-gallows/

—Pittsburgh Post-Gazette (Pittsburgh, Pennsylvania) · Sat, Oct 8, 1977 · Page 21 Some Old Ghost Tales

**Moll Derry:**
—The Evening Standard Uniontown, Pennsylvania Friday, July 02, 1976 - Page 51.
—Ellis, F. E. (1882). History of Fayette County Pennsylvania.
—maryoldmollderry - derrysinamerica2. (n.d.). Retrieved from —
—https://sites.google.com/site/derrysinamerica2/maryoldmollderry

**Polly Williams:**
—Albert, G. D. (1882). History of the County of Westmoreland, Pennsylvania: With Biographical Sketches of Many of Its Pioneers and Prominent Men.
—Hadden, J. (1913). A History of Uniontown: The County Seat of Fayette County, Pennsylvania.
—Hill, A. F. (1865). The White Rocks: Or, The Robbers' Den. A Tragedy of the Mountains.
—PA Room: Digital Bookshelf – Uniontown Public Library. (n.d.). Retrieved from https://uniontownlib.org/pa-shelf/
—History of Fayette County, Pennsylvania : with biographical sketches of many of its pioneers and prominent men : Ellis, Franklin, 1828-1885 : Free Download, Borrow, and Streaming : Internet Archive. (n.d.). Retrieved from https://archive.org/details/historyoffayette00elli/page/n721/mode/2up/search/polly+williams
—Map of Fayette County, Pennsylvania : from actual surveys. (n.d.). Retrieved from https://www.loc.gov/resource/g3823f.la000747/?r=0.285,0.371,0.114,0.042,0
—Murder by Gaslight. (2013, January 19). Retrieved from https://www.murderbygaslight.com/2012/12/cut-off-in-her-youthful-bloom.html
—"Polly Williams Murder of 1810 Recalled in Area." The Morning Herald [Uniontown] 20 Aug. 1957: 1. (n.d.).
—Polly Williams. (n.d.). Retrieved from https://www.findagrave.com/memorial/5936006/polly-williams
—Swetnam, George. The Evening Standard Uniontown, Pennsylvania Wednesday, May 05, 1937 - Page 3 Weird Story of Polly Williams' Tragic Death Told. (n.d.).
—Van Kirk, Jean. The Morning Herald Uniontown, Pennsylvania February 10, 1958 - Page 89 Polly Williams in Tragic Love. (n.d.).

**Fort Necessity:**
—https://www.history.com/news/george-washington-french-indian-war-jumonville
—https://www.nps.gov/fone/battle.htm Battle of Fort Necessity.
—http://www.panicd.com/fort-necessity-national-battlefield.html
—ABOUT US - Trail History - GREAT ALLEGHENY PASSAGE. https://gaptrail.org/about-us/trail-history

**Braddock's Grave:**
—http://www.panicd.com/braddocks-grave.html
—https://www.nps.gov/fone/braddockgrave.htm

**Iron Bridge:**
—Craig Blackwell - Finding James Finley's Chain Bridge over Jacob's Creek. youtube.com/watch?v=tnCEoMGX59o&feature=relmfu
—The Philadelphia Inquirer September 15, 1923 - Page 12
—History of Fayette County Franklin Ellis 1882
—The Morning Herald Uniontown Pa January 3, 1920 Find Woman's Body in Jacob's Creek
—The Daily Courier March 15, 1912—http://www.histbuffer.com/2015/10/ghosts-banshees-and-witches.html

**Rices Landing and Stovepipe:**
—Haunted History. (n.d.). Retrieved from https://www.facebook.com/historyhaunted/photos/history-haunting-of-horse-shoe-bend-rices-landing-pennsylvania-usastovepipe-trai/922887657737315/
—Venable, W. (n.d.). Retired Professor Recounts History of Rices Landing. Retrieved from https://www.uppermon.org/news/Other/OR-Rices_Landing-2Feb12.html
—YouTube Video by Chip - Horseshoe Bend in Rices Landing,PA. (n.d.). Retrieved from https://www.youtube.com/watch?v=7uQ6Oq5rPAw
—23 Jul 2006, Page 119 - Pittsburgh Post-Gazette at Newspapers.com. (n.d.).
—Haunted History. (n.d.). Retrieved from https://www.facebook.com/historyhaunted/photos/history-haunting-of-horse-shoe-bend-rices-landing-pennsylvania-usastovepipe-trai/922887657737315/
—Rosemary Ellen Guiley and Kevin Paul. (2018). Haunted Hills and Hollows: What Lurks in Greene County, Pennsylvania. Visionary Living.

**Shades of Death Road:**
—Geocaching. (n.d.). Shades Of Death. Retrieved from https://www.geocaching.com/geocache/GC4VQAT_shades-of-death?guid=e9240144-3d6f-4005-baa8-94045f969b26
—Pittsburgh Post-Gazette Pittsburgh, Pennsylvania Wednesday, January 11, 1939 - Page 13.
—The Riot of Cliftonville. (2019, July 16). Retrieved from https://www.heinzhistorycenter.org/blog/discover-meadowcroft/riot-of-cliftonville

**Mad Anthony Wayne:**
—Kevin Cuneo / Contributing writer. (n.d.). Kevin Cuneo: 'Mad' Anthony Wayne's story has it all. Retrieved from https://—www.goerie.com/entertainmentlife/20180726/kevin-cuneo-mad-anthony-waynes-story-has-it-all
—Norfolk, S., & Norfolk, B. (2014). The Virginia Giant: The True Story of Peter Francisco. Charleston, SC: Arcadia Publishing

**Presque Isle Storm Hag:**
—10 Creepy Urban Legends From Pennsylvania Not For The Faint Of Heart. (2015, April 1). Retrieved from https://www.onlyinyourstate.com/pennsylvania/pa-urbanlegends/
—Retrieved from http://www.examiner.com/examiner/x-4872-Pittsburgh-Paranormal-Examiner~y2009m4d17-The-Lake-Erie-

Storm-Hag-demonic-siren-of-the-Great-Lakes
—Hunting for shipwrecks in Presque Isle's Misery Bay. (2018, March 8). —
—Retrieved from http://www.rockthelake.com/buzz/2018/02/hunting-for-shipwrecks-in-presque-isles-misery-bay/
—Jenny Green Teeth : Internet Archive. (n.d.). https://archive.org/details/donald_002
—The Lake Erie 'Storm Hag', demonic siren of the Great Lakes. (n.d.). Retrieved from http://theparanormalpastor.blogspot.com/2009/04/lake-erie-storm-hag-demonic-siren-of.html
—Nearby Attractions to Erie Bluffs State Park. https://www.dcnr.pa.gov/StateParks/FindAPark/ErieBluffsStatePark/Pages/NearbyAttractions.aspx

**Zombie Land:**
—The Strange History Behind America's Creepiest Zombie Road Legends... And How You Can Find Them. (2016, July 16). Retrieved from https://weekinweird.com/2011/09/26/home-zombie-roads/
—This time, Zombie Land tale is true. (n.d.). Retrieved from https://old.post-gazette.com/regionstate/20001031zombie1.asp
—Zombie Land, Hillsville, PA. (n.d.). Retrieved from https://zombielandhillsville.blogspot.com/2015/10/

**Hell's Hollow:**
—29 Oct 1977, 23 - Pottsville Republican at Newspapers.com. (n.d.).
—Brown, R. (1888). History of Mercer County, Pennsylvania: Its Past and Present, Including ... Portraits and Biographies of Pioneers and Representative Citizens ; Statistics, Etc. ; Also, a Condensed History of Pennsylvania.
—Hell's Hollow Wildlife Adventure Trail. (n.d.). Retrieved from https://www.visitpa.com/region/pennsylvanias-great-lakes-region/hells-hollow-wildlife-adventure-trail
—Robert-P-Worst - User Trees - Genealogy.com. (n.d.). Retrieved from https://www.genealogy.com/ftm/w/o/r/Robert-P-Worst/WEBSITE-0001/UHP-1251.html

**Crow Rock:**
—Retrieved from https://www.ancestry.com/boards/thread.aspx?mv=flat&m=11335&p=localities.northam.usa.states.pennsylvania.counties.greene
—The Recalling of an Indian Tragedy By Rev. R. Frank Getty, in Presbyterian Banner, Nov. 12, 1906 . (n.d.).
—The History of Marshall County, West Virginia 1879.
—Nyland, Danielle. Investigating Crow Rock. Greenespace Magazine.
—https://www.geni.com/people/Susannah-Crow/6000000031510310010
—Indian Settler Conflicts - WVGenWeb. http://www.wvgenweb.org/marshall/indian.htm

**Hill View Manor:**
—https://ellwoodcity.org/2016/10/10/haunted-hillview-manor/
—https://www.hauntedrooms.com/pennsylvania/haunted-places/hill-view-manor-new-castle

www.ingramcontent.com/pod-product-compliance
Lightning Source LLC
Chambersburg PA
CBHW050826180626

46814CB00004B/1486